"Sweet William rose on a merry May morn," she sang, just barely aloud, putting her lips down close to his cheek. This was not a May morn; it was actually late February, but that didn't matter. It was the name "Sweet William" in the song that mattered, because that meant him.

"Sweet William rose on a merry May morn
And dressed himself in blue
Set himself astride his milk-white steed
Rode off to his love so true—"

The verses of the old ballad got pretty grim, Mama told him. Sweet William had a hard row to hoe, she said, before his story was ended, and so she made up new words, not bothering with the rhymes, just rambling on in a singsong about things that would make William smile, that would brush all the sleepiness out of his eyes and get him ready for his morning chores.

Tempo Books by Irene Hunt

ACROSS FIVE APRILS
THE LOTTERY ROSE
NO PROMISES IN THE WIND
UP A ROAD SLOWLY
WILLIAM

William

IRENE HUNT

TEMPO BOOKS, NEW YORK

0101841116

This Tempo Book contains the complete
text of the original hardcover edition.
It has been completely reset in a typeface
designed for easy reading, and was printed
from new film.

WILLIAM

A Tempo Book / published by arrangement with
Charles Scribner's Sons

PRINTING HISTORY
Scribner's edition / 1977
First Tempo edition / November 1978
Third printing / January 1984

ISBN: 0-441-88981-6

Tempo Books are published by The Berkley Publishing Group,
200 Madison Avenue, New York, New York 10016.
Tempo Books are registered in the United States Patent Office.
PRINTED IN THE UNITED STATES OF AMERICA

one

HER VOICE was part of his morning dream, part of the blanket of sleep he tried to draw up around his ears and hold on to for another hour or so. He heard it though, the low singing that meant breakfast was ready, and the sun was up; that there was work to be done on a Saturday morning when he was free from school.

First he must drag a ladder out of the tool-shed and climb to the tops of the six orange trees that hadn't been "picked over" during the evenings after school throughout the week. There were still several bushels of oranges out there which Mr. Cooper would buy for his produce stand when he came past in his truck.

"I'll pay your ma a good price, William, if the oranges are handled gentle—if they're twisted from their stems, not pulled off with holes left for rot to set in—" Mr. Cooper told him.

Well, of course. Nobody who knew anything about oranges was going to yank them off their stems and risk a lot of spoiling before they ever reached the market. William told Mr. Cooper not to worry, that he knew how to handle oranges.

Now Mama was singing to him, singing him awake, singing that it was too bad to wake him so early on a Saturday morning, but all the same there was work to be done and William must be up and at it. The fruit still hanging on the trees meant a little more money for the family; and now that bread and milk and everything cost a lot and Mama wasn't working, they needed all the money they could get.

"Sweet William rose on a merry May morn," she

sang, just barely aloud, putting her lips down close to his cheek. This was not a May morn; it was actually late February, but that didn't matter. It was the name "Sweet William" in the song that mattered, because that meant him. It was a song she had heard when she was little, but she couldn't remember all the verses; nowadays she sang the first one and then made up her own words just for William:

> "Sweet William rose on a merry May morn
> And dressed himself in blue
> Set himself astride his milk-white steed
> Rode off to his love so true—"

The verses of the old ballad got pretty grim, Mama told him. Sweet William had a hard row to hoe, she said, before his story was ended, and so she made up new words, not bothering with the rhymes, just rambling on in a singsong about things that would make William smile, that would brush all the sleepiness out of his eyes and get him ready for his morning chores.

> "Only on this merry May morn—" (she sang)
> "The month is February and not May—
> Instead of dressing himself in his Sunday blue,
> He pulled on a pair of old faded pants,
> Splashed good cold water over his face
> Ate all his grits and scrambled eggs,
> Drank his orange juice, full of Vitamin C
> Kissed his little mama and climbed the highest orange tree."

"You got a pretty good rhyme goin' there at the last, Mama." He smiled as he struggled through sleep that left him limp as Carla's rag doll. He opened his eyes halfway and looked at Mama's black cheeks, velvety cheeks that used to be as round as Amy's, as William's own. Her

2

cheeks seemed to be caving in lately; they plunged into hollows among the laugh lines on either side of her mouth.

"When I'm big as Amy, you can't call me 'Sweet William' anymore, can you, Mama?"

Something twisted in her face for just a second. Then she said, "That's right. Only when we're alone. It's just between the two of us—" She smoothed some hair back from his forehead.

"You used to call Papa that, didn't you?"

"Yes. His name was William too, you know, and he liked sweet-talk the way you do—" She turned away suddenly, and leaning forward, sat for a short time, both arms pressed against her body. The gesture took away all the laziness of a slow waking from William's eyes.

"You're not feelin' so good this morning, huh, Mama?"

"Not just this minute, but I'm going to take some of Dr. Finley's medicine now—that will pep me up in no time." She got up from the side of his bed and stood looking down at him. "Get into your clothes, William. By the time you're dressed and have had your breakfast, I'll feel well enough to hold the ladder for you when you climb up the orange trees—"

"Why don't you make ol' Amy hold the ladder? Can't she do something around here?"

"You mustn't talk like that. Your sister does a lot to help this family get along. She had to draw Carla to town in the little wagon this morning. The blind children are having Saturday classes for the rest of the winter so that they can be dismissed early when the heat gets bad. That four-mile walk to and from town is no fun for Amy—"

Ashamed, William was quiet. He got out of bed when Mama left for the kitchen and after he splashed his face and neck with cold water and dressed, he went out to the screened porch where the table was set for breakfast. A glass of orange juice stood at his plate and his mother moved slowly out from the kitchen, carrying a plate piled with scrambled eggs and toast.

The smell of food made him feel cheerful. "Smells good, Mama; smells real good. Are you havin' breakfast with me?"

"Coffee now. A little something more later."

"When the medicine makes you feel good again?"

"Yes, I'll have some toast before we go to work. Eat your eggs now while they're hot."

"What makes you hurt, Mama?" he persisted. "Mrs. Cooper told Amy the doctors found a sickness inside you when you went to the hospital last year. Did they—or is ever'body just tryin' to scare me lately?"

She waited a second before she answered. "Doctors find sickness in people every day of the year, William. We wish there wasn't such a thing in this world, but there is. We just have to live with it."

"Can't Dr. Finley make your sickness go away?"

"Maybe. We'll see. He's a good doctor."

"He won't let it make you die, will he, Mama?"

She got up to open the screen door for Duchess, the golden retriever, who was scratching impatiently, asking to come inside and share William's breakfast. "We're not going to mention such a thing as dying in front of Duchess," she said smiling as she bent and looked into the dog's brown eyes. "Life's bouncing all around Duchess these days, most of it tugging for her milk. Let's give her the scraps from Amy's and Carla's plates— maybe you can spare her a bite of your eggs?"

Mama's face looked kind of happy again as she rubbed the dog's golden head, and as he watched her, William felt reassured. Maybe the pills Dr. Finley was giving her might just be making her well again. Amy

4

said they wouldn't, but they might. Amy didn't know everything—not by a long shot, she didn't.

"What are we going to do about all your babies, Duchess?" Mama asked the beautiful retriever. "What are we going to do with all those little wrigglers you birthed into this world?"

"She's started to wean them," William said. "She's beginnin' to push the little guys away like she's sick and tired of them—"

"She has a way of knowing when it's time to push them aside. We must find good homes for them pretty soon. Try not to love them too much, William. Hard as it's going to be, we'll have to part with them—"

"Yes, I know. Too many mouths to feed." It had become a habit for him to speak sternly to them each morning when he went out to look at the puppies. "I'll just pass the time of day with you little mutts," he'd tell them. "No cuddlin' you in my hands—no lettin' myself get hurt because I love you too much—"

As they wondered about homes for Duchess's babies that morning, William suddenly thought of their new neighbor, the girl who had dragged a big suitcase and a portable typewriter out to Mary Hand's house next door earlier that week. Mary Hand had talked to Mama on the telephone and she'd said the girl would call as soon as her bus got in. It had all been settled—Mr. Cooper was going to meet the girl in town at the bus station. But no, she didn't call anybody—she just walked the two miles out from town, carrying all that heavy luggage, and then she fainted at the bottom step of Mary Hand's porch. William had been watching her as she came slowly up the walk and he'd seen her fall with her face down flat in the grass. He had run home to call Mama and she came and washed the girl's face in cold water. Then she helped her to rest on the old couch Mary Hand liked to keep on the back porch. Mama had made him go back home, but she stayed and talked to the girl for a long time.

Amy and William had been crazy to hear everything when Mama came home, but she wouldn't talk very much. She said the girl's name was Sarah West and that she was a faraway cousin of Mary Hand. She told them the girl had been living in an orphan place in New York, but she'd run away twice so the orphan people let her go to Albany to live with Mary Hand.

"Then how come she's here?" William had asked, but Mama just shook her head. She said she was tired and would William and Amy please forget about any more questions. And so, of course, they did, but they wondered a lot between themselves.

Now, after a week of watching the girl next door and wondering about her, William got the idea of taking one of the puppies over to her. Maybe she would like that—unless, of course, she was stuck-up and didn't like puppies or people or nothing.

"Do you think the new girl would like to have one of Duchess's little guys if we'd offer her one?" he asked after a while. "That way we'd have it close by."

Mama thought it was a good idea. Company for Sarah. A way to keep at least one of the puppies near enough for William to watch over it. She said, "Yes, that's a neighborly thing to do. Why don't you take one over to her after supper this evening?"

"Unless maybe she's bigheaded and won't want it," William suggested. He hoped that what he said wasn't true, but he was smarting a little because the girl just stayed in Mary Hand's yard drawing pictures or reading—never once looking up to pass the time of day with him.

"She's not bigheaded, William. She's a lonely girl

with lots of troubles on her mind. We have to be pleasant—offer her some of our oranges, tell her we're glad she's living next door to us—"

"Is she going to stay long?" William asked, scraping food from all the plates for Duchess.

"Maybe. Mary has told her that she can stay down here until—until she's well again—"

" 'Til she don't faint anymore, I guess?" His mother didn't answer and so he tried another question.

"Would you say she's mostly kid or mostly grown-up?" he asked.

"Some of both, I guess. Mary says she's a very bright, talented girl—has finished high school with honors and she's just turned sixteen—"

"That's older than Amy, and Amy thinks that thirteen's pretty grown-up. It's not though, is it, Mama?"

"Not very. And eight years plus four months is so young that the nurses down at the hospital can still remember some of the babies who were yelling and screaming there in the nursery a little over eight years ago—"

"You're not talking about me, are you?"

"Yes, I am. Just the other day Miss Barnes stopped me in the hall when I went in to see Dr. Finley. She said, 'How's that little Sweet William baby I whacked across the bottom six or seven years ago?' "

"What did she mean—six or seven years ago?" William asked scornfully.

"That's what I told her. I said, 'Do you realize that baby is an eight-year-old boy now with four months along toward being nine?' "

"And then did she say, 'My, how time flies, Missus Saunders'?"

"Something like that. You know the things big people are apt to say, don't you?"

He was quiet for a while, thinking over some things

he'd heard big people say around the neighborhood lately. Finally he said, "Mrs. Cooper thinks the new girl shouldn't be living in Mary Hand's house by herself. Do you think it's any of Mrs. Cooper's business, Mama?"

"Yes, it is, William. Mrs. Cooper is worried about a young girl living alone among strangers—so am I for that matter. But when Mary phoned me she said that Sarah is used to taking care of herself. Mary thinks as long as Mrs. Cooper and I look after her a little that it's better for Sarah to be here than in Mary's tiny apartment or the orphanage."

"I wish good ol' Mary could come down and live with her," William said thoughtfully. Mary Hand used to spend most of her vacations in her old home, but she hadn't been down for more than a year now. William knew that she was taking care of her father who was very old and feeble. He supposed that was right, but he missed the excitement of having Mary Hand arrive with gifts, of having party food in her kitchen, of hearing her raspy voice talking for hours with Mama out on one front porch or the other.

Even though she couldn't get down often anymore, Mary depended on Mama to keep the house going as if it might be used any week or so. She kept the electricity connected so that Mama could store fruit and vegetables in the big freezer, some for her own family, some for Mary Hand in case she ever needed them. William went over with his mother almost every week and they opened the windows to let fresh air blow through the rooms; if mildew showed up on a wall or the shelves of books on either side of the fireplace, it was William's job to spray and wipe down until everything was fresh again.

Upstairs there were many bedrooms all along either side of the hall, small ones for each of Mary's three sisters and herself, a large one at the end of the hall for their parents, another one for company.

"We used to sneak out into one another's rooms sometimes," Mary Hand told William once. "Maybe we'd want to whisper secrets or finish a quarrel we'd started earlier—maybe it was just because we were supposed to stay in our own rooms and behave ourselves." She smiled when she told him that, and William had laughed. It seemed very funny to think that Mary Hand had ever been a kid or that she'd ever been kind of a mean one like him and Amy.

When Mama occasionally allowed William and Amy to spend the night with Mary Hand they made a big thing of looking over all the rooms and deciding which ones they'd choose. But there was something spooky about so many empty rooms, and so they usually chose ones on either side of Mary Hand and left the doors open between her room and theirs.

Amy kept pots and baskets out on the wide front porch, and unless the weather was stormy, she left the wicker chairs behind the porch rail as Mary used to do when she was expecting company. A boy from town, Robert Norris, came out once a week to cut the grass and trim the bushes when they needed it. Mama had done that for a long time with William's help. Not anymore.

Mary Hand's place looked nice. So did the smaller house next door, the house that long ago had been used to take care of an overflow of guests when Mary and her sisters were grown-up girls. The Hands hadn't had that much company in a long time though, Mary said; and so she had been glad to sell the smaller house and the acre of ground that had been cleared from the edge of the pine woods that rose big and dark behind the two houses. Papa bought the "company house" when he and Mama were first married; he'd added more bedrooms and screened porches back and front when his family began to grow larger. It was a nice place, William thought, with a green lawn in front, with flower and vegetable gardens in the back.

Mary Hand was a lot older than Mama, but that didn't matter; they liked one another and Mama said they always had. She told Amy and William that Mary Hand was as nice to her as Mama's own mother would have been, and once when she overheard William mimicking Mary's scratchy voice, he got his legs switched. Remembering, William didn't blame Mama for the switching—it had been a mean, cussed thing for him to do.

Mary Hand wasn't very pretty. Her long white face made her look a little like one of Mr. Cooper's palomino horses; but then, so what? William loved the palominos, and, anyway, Mary Hand was good. Sometimes she made him mad because she liked Amy better than anybody. Sometimes he told himself that Mary Hand made him sick to his stomach with all her goings-on about how pretty Amy was and how Amy was just about her own kid and blah, blah. But then, maybe the next minute Mary would find a present she'd brought him from New York or maybe she'd take him to town in her car for an ice-cream cone, and then he'd like her again.

That morning at breakfast Mama explained some more about Mary liking Amy so much. "She took Amy over to her house and cared for her six months or more when I wasn't well," she told him. "Some women get to loving babies they care for the way you get to loving a puppy that looks to you for its food and some petting—"

"Did she like me when I was a baby later on?" he asked, knowing the answer, but wanting Mama's words to iron out the wrinkle of jealousy inside him.

"You know very well how much Mary loved you." She gave him a look that told him he'd asked a silly question, then a minute later she ruffled up his hair and smiled at him. "Mary always said your eyes were just like mine—"

"Are they, Mama?" he asked, pleased.

"Um-m, somewhat. I'd say yours are a little prettier—"

"No, they're not. There ain't any eyes prettier than yours."

She laughed then, almost the way she used to when she teased him a lot. "All right, young man, but all those nice words in your mouth are not going to keep you out of our orange trees this morning. Come on, let's get to work."

He pushed his chair back and ran quickly to the shed where the ladder and orange crates were stored. He showed off a little by climbing to the very top of the first tree and stepping over to an outgrowing branch where he could stretch himself to reach the highest oranges. He had a canvas bag tied around his waist and when it was full, he'd hand it down to Mama so she could pour the oranges from it into one of the crates Mr. Cooper had left for them.

His mother was frightened when he climbed so high. "Be careful, William—oh, do be careful," she called to him. She hadn't always been so fearful. Even a year ago when he was only a few months past seven she hadn't been so much afraid that he'd get hurt.

"Don't worry, Mama. I'm a surefooted mountain goat. I'm a crazy old mountain goat that somehow got caught up in this orange tree."

He laughed at that idea and his mother smiled. Amy would have said, "Not funny, smart aleck," but Mama didn't. She just said, "Well, stay surefooted, mountain goat. Your mama doesn't want to hear any little goat crying with broken bones or hurts inside him."

They worked without saying much for a couple of hours after that. After a while William gave up being a show-off as weariness set in, and he noticed that his mother looked tired too.

"I think I'll have to rest for a while now, William," she said finally. "Please don't get up on the high branches until Amy comes to help you." She looked up at him earnestly. "Give me your word—then I can rest without worrying—"

He nodded. "I'll mind you, Mama. There's plenty of oranges lower down to keep me busy—"

She walked slowly toward the house and he thought how quick she got tired these days, not like she used to be when she typed Mr. Hager's letters for him in town all day and then came home to cook and work in the garden and put vegetables and fruit in Mary Hand's freezer. Sometimes he forgot to notice how tired Mama got— then all at once he'd think about it and feel worried deep inside somewhere.

Amy came home about ten and she offered to climb the ladder and spell him for a while. As he watched her, he felt ashamed again that he'd said she didn't do much of anything. It wasn't that he didn't like Amy; it was just that somehow they were always getting in one another's hair. But it had been mean of him to talk smart against Amy; that four-mile walk to and from town was quite a chore in the hot sun, and now here she was helping him with the oranges so that he could have a rest.

"I'll go in and get Carla this afternoon," he said. Amy just shrugged her shoulders; she might have said "All right, thank you" the way Mama had raised her to answer a nice word from anyone. But she didn't.

At noon they sat on the grass and shared an orange which William divided with his pocket knife. "Mama says we can give the new girl next door one of Duchess's puppies," William remarked as he spat some orange seeds on the ground beside him.

Amy got mad easily. "Duchess is my dog, same as yours—I guess I have something to say about handin' over one of her puppies to this new girl—" she snapped.

"Well, then, go ahead and have something to say about it. Don't you want one of the puppies kept close by where we can keep an eye on it? Or do you want all of them to go somewhere far off with strangers?"

"I just don't like for you and Mama to make up your minds without saying a word to me about it—"

"Oh, we didn't. We thought to ourselves that we better ask Amy about this because Amy is the big shot around here, and even Mama better not make up her mind without bowing to Missus Amy and saying, 'Can we, your Royal Highness?' "

"Shut up," Amy said, but she grinned a little and wasn't quite so mad.

"If we give her a puppy, that's being neighborly," he explained, "and we're supposed to be neighborly 'cause she's got some kind of trouble on her mind." He thought he was giving Amy a piece of news, but instead of looking interested, she looked high and mighty.

"I know what her trouble is," Amy said, raising her brows slightly. "Some girls in town told me and they know because their mothers told them about it."

"I bet you're lying," he told her.

"I'm not either. I know exactly what kind of trouble is on her mind."

"Then tell me—what kind of trouble is it?"

"I won't talk about it. Little kids aren't supposed to know."

"Yeah. I thought so. You don't know or you couldn't keep your mouth shut about it. You're telling a great big lie when you say you know so much."

"All right then, I'll tell you. That girl's going to have a baby. And she's got trouble on her mind because that baby's not going to have a papa."

William looked at his sister, puzzled. "What's so much trouble about that? Duchess had *six* babies and they don't have a papa."

Amy could look very prim when she tried being grown-up. "Oh, William, you're such a child," she said, sounding like Mrs. Cooper.

Quickly he had an answer for her. "Oh, Amy, you're such a smart-ass," he shot back.

"Wait 'til I tell Mama what you said, William Saunders. You remember the scolding you got for saying 'son of a bitch' when the mailman swore at Duchess." Amy looked like, well! she certainly had the goods on William this time.

He fixed that look though. He said, "All right, go ahead. If you like to worry Mama when the medicine's not makin' her feel good—well, then, do it. Go ahead and worry her."

Amy was suddenly thoughtful. "No," she said. After a minute they moved closer together and sat there without saying anything for a long time.

They worked on the oranges until almost four; then William went into town to pick up four-year-old Carla at the special school for the blind.

Carla was not completely blind. She knew when it was daylight or when the lamps were turned on at night. She could see the movement of an arm being lifted and lowered; she could see that a refrigerator was big and a step stool was small. But let William and Amy sit side by side without speaking and Carla could not tell one from the other. She couldn't see colors or the pictures in the storybooks Mama read to her. The word "blind" was one that Amy and William and Mama hated to say, but they had to face the truth: Carla was almost completely blind, and all they could do was to take her to the special class for the blind and hope that she would learn the things other children learned in nursery school and kindergarten.

Carla had screamed at first, terrified because Mama went away and left her with strangers. But when kindness from teachers who understood her fear had made her feel secure, Carla liked going into town with Amy and William each school day, feeling that she was growing up, no longer a baby who had to stay at home all day. At supper she liked to show Mama how she had learned to eat without spilling food on her dress, and if Mama had to go to bed early, Carla would sit close beside her, retelling all the stories and nursery rhymes she'd learned during the day. She made Amy and William join her in playing the new games she'd learned, and when Mr. Cooper dropped by to visit with the family, Carla would climb on his lap and the two of them would sing the funny old songs Mr. Cooper had learned when he was as little as Carla.

Now, on Saturday when he had come to take Carla home, William waited in the hall until Mrs. Parr led his sister down to meet him. William liked Mrs. Parr. Sometimes she talked to him about some of Carla's problems, almost as if she thought he was as old as Mama. "Carla trusts you, William. You are very important to your little sister," she told him once.

Carla was bouncy and frisky as she climbed into her wagon and waved good-bye to her teacher. She was, as usual, eager to tell William all about her day, even about that part of it when she had been naughty.

"What did you do that was bad, Carla?" William asked as he started pulling the small express wagon down the road.

"Mostly I guess I talked too much," Carla said carelessly. "I wasn't really bad, William—Mrs. Parr is just a fuss-button about talking."

"Mrs. Parr is awfully nice to you, Carla. Can't you cut down on the talking a little next week?" William asked.

"No, I don't think so." Carla was serious for a minute. "I have lots of things to say and the only way I can say all of them is to talk too much." She smiled then and turned her face up to William. "Want to hear me sing a song Mr. Cooper taught me?" she asked.

Her voice was sweet, a little shrill when she got carried away in her pleasure at having an audience, but it was clear and sounded pretty in the still, sundown part of the day. She swayed in her wagon slightly as she sang.

> *"I got a hook and you got a line—Honey,*
> *I got a hook and you got a line—Babe!*
> *I got a hook and you got a line,*
> *Gonna catch a crawdad sure this time,*
> *Honey, Oh, Honey-Babe!"*

"You like that song, William?" she asked as soon as her lips had smacked over the final word "Babe" in the last line.

"Yeah, that's real good, Carla. Makes me wish I had a recorder so I could tape your singing—"

"Well, you make some money real quick and buy one." She laughed and bounced around in her wagon so full of energy William was afraid she might fall over the wheels. "Want me to sing about the old gray mare that ain't what she used to be?" she asked.

"Sure, that's a good one. I'll sing it with you," he said.

And so they sang together the rest of the way home, Carla choosing one song after another, each one getting a little louder than the one just finished. When they got to the gate at home, Mama was standing there waiting for them.

"I've been hearing you since you were a half-mile up the road," she said. "It sounded so good I had to come out where I could hear you better." She was laughing as she lifted Carla out of the wagon and kissed her, and her laughing made William feel that everything in the world was all right for the time, that he hadn't a thing to worry about.

As soon as William and Carla had washed the dust from their hands and faces, they all went out on the porch where Amy had put supper on the table.

"This is a nice meal you've fixed for us, Amy-girl," Mama said. William thought, well, he couldn't quite buy that. The fried potatoes were burned on one side and the stewed tomatoes were too watery. Still, Amy had done her best he supposed, and certainly he wasn't going to say anything to make her mad again. He wanted to take his gift over to the girl in Mary Hand's house after supper without getting into any more arguments with Amy.

"Is it all right with you, Amy, if I take one of Duchess's puppies over next door after supper?" he asked. He tried pretty hard to be friendly.

Amy was tired, not in a good mood. "You're so polite it must be an awful strain on you," she said, shrugging her shoulders. "About the puppy—that's up to you and Duchess—"

He had it in his mind to say "Well thanks for nothin'," but something in the way his mother looked at him gave him a change of mind. He helped Mama with the dishes as soon as supper was over and then hurried outside to see if Duchess had any idea that he was about to give away one of her children. She had been very savage about anyone coming near them at first, but William had a feeling that after six weeks of putting up with their greedy tugging for milk and their sharp-toothed nips at her belly, Duchess might not mind giving up a few or even all of her puppies.

Duchess had been the runt of the litter of purebred golden retrievers four years ago, such a weakly runt that the man who owned her mother thought that Duchess didn't amount to much and let William's father buy her for almost nothing. But maybe because Amy and William loved her so much, Duchess had grown healthier and she had whelped strong well-formed puppies, lively and smart, but most of them looking very unlike Duchess.

In the present litter though, there were two golden balls for fur almost exactly like her except that they were larger and sturdier than she had been as a puppy. It was one of these bright youngsters that William chose for the girl in Mary Hand's house.

"I'm taking this one over to the new girl, Duchess. You needn't worry, you'll get to see your baby every day. And right now there's one less to hurt your poor sore titties—" He stroked her head tenderly and Duchess closed her eyes in contentment. It was plain that William was welcome to do whatever he liked with her family.

He walked a little way into the woods, putting off his visit with the new girl for just a while. At supper he'd been eager to get over and talk to her; now, he wasn't so sure. Somehow it seemed better just to walk in the woods and maybe think a little before he tried to be a good neighbor. The air was soft and the woods were still. Off through the windbreak of Australian pines between their own acre of ground and Mr. Cooper's truck garden he could catch glimpses of the Gulf which looked as big as God out there in the twilight. The woods were a nice place for lingering at that hour.

He walked on slowly, stopping for a minute beside his thinking stone as he always did when he came into the woods this far. It was a great boulder, shaped much like a sleeping frog and covered with moss and lichens. William remembered the day his father had pointed it out to him and they decided it should be called William's thinking stone.

William had been mad that day, mad at Mama of all people, but then he was young at the time and Mama had scolded him because he'd been mean to Amy. Not only scolded him, but she'd taken away his toy dump trucks too, and that's why he was mad and running away. He was running and crying and talking to himself between sobs when his father suddenly overtook him.

"You going somewhere, William?" Papa had asked. He took out a handkerchief and wiped the tears out of William's eyes and the sweat off his face. He said, "Let's sit here and have a little visit together, shall we?" And that was the first time William could remember the big boulder.

"This would make a good thinking stone for you." Papa had put his arm around William's shoulder. "Lots of people need thinking stones," he said after a while. I have one about three miles from here on the shore of a little lake beyond the woods. This one could be yours if you want it."

"What good is it?" William had wanted to know, and Papa said such a stone could be a lot of good if it belonged to the right person. He said some people couldn't get any good out of a stone, but there were others who liked one to sit on—to be by themselves and think about things that made them mad or worried them or hurt their feelings. It even made a good place to sit and smile and say "Praise the Lord" when something good happened and they were full of joy.

Plenty of times, Papa said, when he was worried about work or little Carla's eyes or about Amy and William fighting one another, he'd go out to his thinking stone and sit there listening to the sound of the woods around him until he could get some plans going inside his mind. Then he'd feel better, ready to go home, and talk things over with little Mama.

"It's better than running away," Papa told him, "mainly because running away would make so many people back home feel lonesome and worried, it might even make the person who ran away feel hungry and scared when night comes."

They had sat on the boulder for a long time that day, close together and not talking much, but liking one another. Once Papa said, "A boy could climb up on this old frog and pretend it's his riding horse, couldn't he?"

That's when William asked, "Will we ever have a horse for Amy and me to ride?" and Papa had said, "I think so. As soon as I can save a little more money I'll talk to Mr. Cooper about buying one of his palomino colts."

That's what Papa would have done too, William thought, if the accident hadn't happened at work.

William had been so busy with his thoughts that he hadn't seen the girl come out into Mary Hand's yard. Now he looked up and saw her walking around the bushes and vines that covered the wicket fence, stopping sometimes to pull some weeds or to look at the hibiscus blooms that were folding up as night got nearer. She looked lonesome, William thought, and he smiled as he glanced down at the puppy in his hands.

"Anybody that's lonesome is going to like you," he said. Then he walked quickly out of the woods and over toward Mary Hand's house.

two

AT FIRST you might think her face was all eyes, William mused later, remembering how Sarah looked that night. They were large, dark-blue eyes and they gave you a level look that made you wonder had you brushed your hair, was you zipped up in front, had you told a lie once, and could she see right down inside you where the lie had been. Her short thick hair was gold-colored like the puppy's coat, and some of it fell straight across her forehead just above her eyebrows. She was taller than Amy and she somehow seemed much older though she wasn't very big. In her blue shorts and tacky old blouse she looked very thin. If there was a baby inside her you certainly couldn't see where it was hiding. Duchess had looked fat as anything when her puppies were waiting to get born.

She just stood there looking at William like she was waiting to hear what he wanted. He hoped she would say hello and ask him to come inside the yard, but she didn't say anything right away. She just looked at him, and William had a feeling that maybe the best thing would be to turn around and go home. Finally, though, she said, "Are you the little Saunders boy next door?"

"Yes, ma'am," he answered, not very happy to be called little, not too sure that he wanted to start a conversation with this girl at all.

She said, "You don't have to say 'ma'am' to me. My name's Sarah."

"I was raised to say 'ma'am' to older ladies." His voice was cooler than he really felt.

"Have it your way." She smiled for the first time, just

a little hint of a smile as she opened the gate. "Do you want something?" she asked, and he had a good notion to tell her, "No, not a thing—" and walk away. But he didn't. He decided to give her another chance.

"I brought you a present." He walked slowly through the gate and showed her the puppy snuggled in his cupped hands. "This is partly because you're our new neighbor and partly because we won't have to give this one away with the others and never see it again." He decided it was better to tell this girl the whole truth about his gift.

She knelt beside him when he put the puppy on the grass at her feet and gave a short gasp when she looked down at it. "What a perfect little creature," she said barely above a whisper. "What a beautiful golden baby—" She took the puppy in her hands and held it close to her. When it peed on her blouse she didn't get mad, just laughed for the first time and kissed the puppy and acted crazy-happy over it.

"She's a girl puppy," William explained. "I thought you might like to know."

"Girl puppy or boy puppy, this is the nicest present anyone could have given me." Her face was all lit up— happy looking. "I've never had a puppy of my own. Nor a kitten. Nor anything."

All at once William thought of something that might please her. "But you're going to have a baby, aren't you?" he asked brightly.

She stopped laughing. When she spoke, her voice was flat. "As a matter of fact, I am," she said after a few seconds. "I see you've heard about it."

"Some girls in town told Amy. Was it bad of her to tell me?"

"Not at all. It's no secret."

"I guess you'll be glad to have a puppy and a real

baby growing up together," he said, hesitating and yet seeing no real reason why she wouldn't like the suggestion.

"Sounds cozy, but that's not the way it's going to be," she said, her face somehow looking scared and angry and sad—all at the same time.

"I don't know what you mean," William admitted in a low voice, feeling sure he shouldn't ask any more questions and yet wanting terribly to understand what she was talking about.

She looked at him so sternly that he thought she might be going to send him home. Then her lips trembled into a sour-looking smile. "Since you already know so much about me, I may as well tell you that we're not going to have a baby growing up with the puppy. Your mother talked to Dr. Finley for me and I'm giving the baby to a couple in Miami who are after him to find one for them—" She took a deep breath. "That will solve a lot of problems," she added.

William was troubled. "I don't like to think about giving a little baby away to people that don't even know it—" He frowned as he looked up at her.

"It's not exactly a fun thing, I'll admit," she said and added in a voice that showed she had made her mind up, "but it's the only thing to do. That's the way it's going to be."

He thought the matter over for a while. "If you don't want the baby, could we have it?" he asked finally. "I think my mama would like to hold it—" He stopped then at a sudden thought. There was the matter of the sickness the doctors had found in his mother's body. There was also the matter of too many mouths to feed. He realized that his suggestion had been foolish.

Anyway the girl was shaking her head. "No, the baby will have to go far away where I'll never see it, so

I'll never have a chance to get attached to it or change my mind and want to keep it. And the baby must never know there was an idiot-girl named Sarah mixed up in its life—"

"Anybody would be crazy to call you an idiot-girl—"

"That's right, isn't it? Completely ridiculous." She grinned at him suddenly and looked friendly again. "What do you say we talk about you for a while, shall we?"

"What things about me do you want to talk about?"

"Well, for a beginning—is your name William?"

"Yes. William Morrison Saunders—same name as my papa's."

She nodded. "Nice dignified name. Mary Hand told me about you—I'd sort of forgotten." Sitting cross-legged on the ground, she allowed the puppy to run back and forth across her knees. "Does your mother call you 'Sweet William' sometimes like the Sweet William in an old English ballad?"

"Yes." He said the word shortly, and the girl looked up at him as if his short answer surprised her.

"You don't like to be called that name?" she asked.

"It's all right for my mama to call me that, but it's just between her and me."

She nodded as if what he said pleased her instead of making her mad. "You're right, of course. It's none of my business. I apologize—"

In spite of her words, William had an uneasy feeling that he had been rude. "I might tell you about it someday—if we get to be good friends," he added.

"Good. We'll wait and see how we get along. I have a feeling that things are going to be all right between us—" William felt pleased about that—a little embarrassed, but pleased. "I heard your typewriter a-goin' yesterday " he remarked, reaching out for something to say.

"You'll hear it a lot from now on. I'm trying to brush up on the typing I had in high school so I can get a job later this year. Your mother thinks maybe I can get the job she used to have—" When she spoke of his mother, Sarah's face grew sober. "She is very good to me, William. Mary Hand would never have let me come down here alone if your mother hadn't agreed to be a good friend to me—"

"Yes, she's a right nice lady." William coughed a small, polite cough. He didn't want to say too much. He didn't care to tell this strange girl that he loved Mama 'til the love went sharp inside him when he saw the pain in her face.

There was another silence between them after that and when it had gone on so long it became embarrassing, William tried again to find something they might talk about.

"Are you glad to be here in Mary Hand's house?" he asked finally.

Sarah placed both hands on the ground behind her and leaned back, looking up at the shuttered windows and at the red brick walls covered with climbing ivy. "Yes, I like it," she said thoughtfully. "Of course it's not the dream I used to have of being here because—well, because of a lot of things—" Her face was sober, but after a while she smiled a little—though the smile, William thought, didn't make her face look happy.

"I've dreamed of coming down to Mary Hand's old house since I was a very little girl," she told William after a time. "My father used to tell me about having Christmas dinner out on this lawn when he was a boy— about flowers blooming in January and fruit still hanging on the trees in February. He used to tell me that some-day we'd come down here and live through a long winter together, that we'd paint on every sunny day and live on nectarines and avocados—"

"You'd soon have wanted a hamburger," William told her.

"Of course we would have. But at the time nectarines and avocados sounded beautiful."

"I could bring you some nectarines," William offered eagerly. "Maybe some avocados too if Mr. Cooper has some leftover ones that are too ripe for him to sell."

She shook her head. "Those things don't matter that much now. They were just a part of a dream that called for my father being here with me."

"Is he the one that showed you how to draw?"

"Yes, he was a great painter and a great teacher. Lots of people are praising his work now—it just about tears me up to think they had to wait until he died before they could appreciate him."

"Did he meet up with an accident like my papa did?" William asked, his eyes wide with sympathy.

She hesitated a few seconds, then she said, "No. No, he didn't have an accident."

"Where's your mama at, Sarah?" He realized that he had called her "Sarah," but no matter. It somehow seemed more natural.

"I don't know," she answered very quietly. "I'm not acquainted with the lady."

He had asked too many questions and he felt ashamed. Nosey. That was what people called it. Mama had warned him that asking too many questions can make people stop liking you. In a voice as low as Sarah's he said, "I didn't mean to be nosey."

Right away her face was friendly again. She said, "Don't worry. A few minutes ago I asked too many questions. Now we're even." She held the puppy up in front of her face and turned to William. "What shall we name this little gold nugget? Or have you already given her a name?"

He shook his head. "Mama didn't want us to name the puppies or pet them for fear we'd get to likin' them so much it would hurt to give 'em away—"

She drew a quick breath, then put her cheek down against the puppy's head. She said, "Yes, if they're to be given away it's better not to know them too well—certainly not to love them."

William didn't pay much attention to her words. He was thinking about a name for the puppy. "What you called her just now sounded good to me—you said, 'little gold nugget.' "

Sarah looked interested. "That's right. It does sound good, doesn't it?" She set the puppy down on the grass between them. "All right, little lady, that's your name—Nugget. From now on when either William or I yell 'Nugget,' you're supposed to come running on the double-quick—"

They laughed together and called Nugget by her new name a dozen times or more as she scampered from one lap to another. After a while they went inside and found a plastic clothes basket and an old quilt to make a bed inside it. At William's suggestion they located an alarm clock upstairs and he wrapped it in a corner of the blanket. "We'll put it close to her tonight—maybe she'll think the ticking is Duchess's heart beatin' and she won't be so lonesome."

When Nugget was laid, fast asleep, in her basket and William had explained to Sarah how to feed and care for her new pet, they went into Mary Hand's living room where large sheets of drawing paper lay scattered over the floor. They were covered with sketches and drawings

Sarah had been working on during the days when she hadn't looked up to speak to an interested neighbor.

William lifted one picture after another and examined them with wonder. There was a corner of the pine woods looking dim and misty as if either early morning or late twilight had touched the tall pines with something dark and mysterious; there was one of rain beating down from an overcast sky and running in narrow rivers down the green kitchen door; then in contrast, there was a brightly colored one of Mary Hand's yard full of sunlight and flowering bushes.

Some of the sketches he glanced at and laid aside quickly—faces that didn't quite look like faces, roughly drawn as they were with heavy black lines: others were only great splashes of color that didn't make sense to William. He wondered that Sarah would waste her time with them.

Sometimes, however, underneath a pile of the meaningless drawings, he'd find something that pleased him. One was made up of only a few lines, but it was plainly a road winding between pine trees and palmettos on its way toward town, and far away there were dim outlines of a boy drawing a little girl in a wagon. "Me and Carla," he exclaimed, delighted.

She nodded and then took up a large painting that had been propped up against the wall. "This is my father," she said, setting the painting high on the mantel above the fireplace. "I took it out of its frame so I could bring it with me—" She stepped back beside William to look at the man who sat slouched on a bench in some park, his long legs stretching out in front of him, his head thrown back and resting against his clasped hands.

He was a lot like Sarah, though his hair was darker—light brown instead of gold like hers—and his cheeks and chin were covered by a soft-looking beard. His eyes were large and had the same level look in them that Sarah's had. There was a smile at the corners of his mouth—a smile that mocked you a little bit and seemed to say, "If you like me, all right; if you don't I couldn't care less."

"Did you make that picture too?" William asked, not quite believing it was possible.

"Yes, I painted it last year, partly as I remembered him, partly with the help of an old photograph," she answered. "It isn't very good, really, but I'll paint a better one later on. I'm learning all the time—"

After a while William went back to the half-finished sketches lying on the floor. He picked up the one of himself and Carla out on the road. "Could I take this one to show Mama and Amy?" he asked. "I'll bring it back tomorrow—"

"Of course. If you'd like I can finish it for you in a few days."

He nodded and moved reluctantly toward the door. A good neighbor shouldn't wear out his welcome—Mama used to tell him and Amy that when they came over to visit with Mary Hand—but he hated to leave. Then, as if she knew how he felt, she opened the sliding doors leading out to the north porch and spoke to him quietly. "Shall we sit out here and watch the woods for a while before it gets too dark?" At that he nodded happily and they sat together on the highest step, not saying anything—just watching the shadows close in around the crowd of high pines that stretched far out toward the Gulf. Once Sarah smiled at him and whispered, "Listen," and he did, leaning forward the better to catch the sounds of soft cracklings and scuttlings, slow movements of branches, one against the other. Once in a while there was a shrill cry out there that made him wonder—was something in the darkness hurt or scared? Or just mad and giving another something a sharp scolding?

He was pleased that Sarah would sit beside him, so relaxed and still, seeming glad to have him there with her. The girls who came out from town to visit Amy were giggly and gabby—they never for a minute stopped and looked away into the woods and listened the way Sarah did.

After a while he said, "A woods is a good place, isn't it?"

Sarah nodded. "I like it," she said quietly.

"Sometimes when you come back here from town you think the woods is the stillest place in the world. But when you listen for a while—"

"Then you're able to hear sounds you've never guessed were out there, aren't you?" She put her hand on his for a second. "If we could turn up the volume of those night sounds, we'd have a woods-orchestra going for us—a whole piney woods symphony right at our back-doors—"

"Yes," he agreed. To himself he thought, I like her. She's going to be my friend. After a while he looked up into her face, "Are you ever lonesome living in this big house by yourself?"

"No," she hesitated for a second, almost as if she weren't quite sure. "Not really lonesome—this is much better than being cooped up with strangers you either don't like or don't care a hoot about. Being alone is not the worst thing in the world—"

"I guess you can keep busy making pictures and working at your typewriter?" he suggested.

"Pretty busy, yes," she said. "And now I have a puppy to look after and when I find time I want to do a little refinishing around here. That stair rail up from the living room is beautiful old wood but it needs sanding and waxing—"

"Couldn't I help you do that?" he asked.

She hesitated a little, then went along with his suggestion. "Yes, I guess you could," she said, "that is, if your mother doesn't mind," she added.

"No, she won't mind." He waited for her to speak again and when she didn't he got to his feet reluctantly. "Well, I guess I'd better be makin' tracks toward home," he said, quoting Mr. Cooper. Then remembering the ways of puppies who miss their mothers, he said, "I hope Nugget won't give you too much trouble tonight—"

"I'll rock her to sleep if she cries," Sarah said, getting up to stand beside him. "It's going to be good having another living creature in the house with me tonight—"

"You're not afraid at night, are you?"

"Not really. Just a bit jumpy when I hear noises I'm not sure about."

"Amy and me could take turns coming over and staying with you if you want us to—"

"No, that would be asking too much of you. I'll tell you what I *will* do though—I'll move a cot and Nugget's basket into the kitchen tonight where we'll be closer to your house. We'll feel better that way—" She held out her hand in a gesture he liked. "Thank you for my puppy, William," she said gravely. "She's a beautiful present."

He nodded and choked with the effort of finding the right words to answer her. "That's OK," he said finally and then he ran across the yard toward home, stopping once to wave back at her.

three

ALL OF THE oranges had been picked by the end of February and Mr. Cooper paid Mama a fancy price for them when he came to haul the last crates away to his produce stand. He liked the careful way William and Amy had handled the oranges and he told Mama he'd never seen bigger fruit or tasted sweeter.

Mama took the check Mr. Cooper gave her and looked at it for a long time without speaking. Then she put it away in an inner pocket of her purse and told William to find Amy and ask her to come into the living room, that she wanted to talk to both of them that evening. So William banged on Amy's door and she yelled, couldn't he show her a little courtesy by knocking; but she calmed down in a few minutes and came out without any more sputtering to sit beside Mama on the couch.

"I want to talk to you children about how we're to manage in the days to come," Mama said after a minute. "Now that I'm not able to work for Mr. Hager we don't have any income except once in a while a check like the one Mr. Cooper just gave me and a small amount which the government pays us because Papa paid into Social Security during the years he worked—"

"Are we awful poor, Mama?" William asked in a low voice.

She smiled at him. It was a weak smile, but it reassured him. "We don't have much, William, that's a fact—but we're not wretchedly poor either. We'll be able to get along if we are careful. That's what I want to talk to you children about this evening—" She looked around the room at the satiny striped wallpaper she had hung by herself before the sickness struck her and at the windows covered by thin curtains she had let Amy help her choose.

"We've got this house, for one thing—there's always a roof over our heads—"

"You've made this place look so nice, Mama," Amy said, putting her hand on Mama's. "I love our little house—"

Mama nodded, but it was plain she had something else on her mind. After a minute she began to speak, more to herself than to him and Amy, William thought. "Mr. Hager has all our important papers—deeds and insurance papers. He'll always look after any money that is due you—there's still a little left of what the company paid us after Papa's accident and there will be small Social Security checks—"

"But you'll do all those things, Mama. You'll look after money the way you always have—" The terror climbing up in William's throat threatened to cut off his breath.

"Yes, honey—yes, of course, I will." Mama's voice was soothing. "It's just that I'm not as strong as I used to be, and so I may have to depend more and more on Mr. Hager to manage some of our business matters. It's the same with taking care of our garden patch—I'll do what I can, of course, but I may have to depend a lot on you children this next year—"

"You mustn't worry, Mama, we can plant things and take care of them the way we've watched you do," Amy said just above a whisper.

"There may be a time—" Mama was speaking slowly as if she wanted to find exactly the right words—"oh, not soon at all, maybe not for months or even a year—when there will be just the three of you—"

William turned to look at Amy. Her eyes were big

and full of the same fear he could feel inside himself. He wished desperately that Mama wouldn't say these things that seemed to mean she was going to die. He thought he might have to scream if she didn't stop.

Then he felt her arm around his shoulder, holding him close to her. "What I want, above all things, is for you children to stay together—to go on being a family. I don't want to think of your being scattered—or not loving one another—"

She was thinking, William was sure, of how he and Amy were forever fighting one another the way they'd done ever since he could remember. Once he'd heard Mr. Cooper say, "It's normal, Libby—it's the way of kids." And when Mama asked him if he thought William and Amy might grow up hating one another, Mr. Cooper said, "Hell, no. Let some outsider belt into one of 'em and watch the other one come runnin'." He said that Mama wasn't to worry.

Now, William wanted to help Mama stop worrying about the fighting that Mr. Cooper thought was normal. "I'll always be good to Amy, Mama—if she behaves herself," he had to add.

Mama told him yes, that she believed him, and she smiled at him so cheerfully, so much the way she used to smile, that he felt better right away. Then she took up a piece of paper she'd been working on. "I've made a list here of all the vegetables we're going to plant, where we'll put them, some of the things we have to remember in taking care of them. We'll have a good time this summer, the three of us farming and watching things grow— Mr. Cooper will give us advice and so will Robert Norris—"

William brightened at mention of Robert Norris. "Yeah, Robert can help us a lot. He knows more about gardens than practically anybody in town."

"That's right. And then there's Sarah. Sarah and I have had some long talks together. She wants to help us all she can."

"How can *she* help us with the work if she's going to have a baby?" Amy asked scornfully.

"Some exercise is good for her as long as she doesn't over-do it. I helped Papa in our garden up to the day William let me know it was time to go to the hospital and get him into this world—"

William smiled at her. He liked hearing about the days he couldn't remember. It seemed funny to think of himself as a little baby waiting to get born.

Mama went on talking about her plans. "Sarah is interested in gardening—she'll learn quickly, though you'll have to teach her a lot. She actually thought that potatoes grew on the plant above ground instead of underneath."

William guffawed at that, but Amy said, "I can see that she's going to be a big help—"

"You may find out that she *is* a big help, Amy. How about giving her a chance and appreciating the fact that she wants to learn?" Mama's voice was sharp and it put Amy in her place.

Mr. Cooper came over with his tractor on Saturday morning to get the ground broken. William could ride with him that day, he said, but later he'd have to get hoes and rakes in action, have to work up a sweat, Mr. Cooper said.

The week they planted potatoes, Sarah came over every evening as soon as Amy and William got home from school and helped them with the cuttings Mama had got ready for them during the day. They'd carry buckets of cuttings out to the patch south of the house and one of them would make a shallow hole with a hoe, another would drop the cutting and a third would go along and rake plenty of topsoil over the cutting. After a few hours of work, Sarah got a monstrous bucket from Mary Hand's storeroom and filled it so they wouldn't have to make so many trips back to the house to refill their smaller pails. And that was the time Mama got mad.

When she saw Sarah lugging the heavy bucket down the rows, Mama hurried out to the garden. "Do you want to lose that baby, Sarah?" she asked, breathing quickly.

"The thought has occurred to me, Mama," Sarah said in a voice that wasn't quite smarty, but almost. She had taken to calling their mother "Mama" as Amy and William and Carla did, and Mama liked that as a rule. That evening, though, she was mad and she spoke in the kind of voice that would have meant a switch around the legs if Sarah had been William.

"I have an idea the same thought occurred to you when you carried your luggage out from the bus station the day you came, didn't it?"

Sarah didn't exactly answer Mama's question. "But, of course, it didn't work. I guess I have to face the fact that I'm strong as a horse," she added.

Mama just stood still and closed her eyes for a second or two. Then she said, "You don't know the trouble you're trying to make for yourself, Sarah, and for me. I promised Mary Hand I'd do everything I could for you, but I'm not strong enough to see you through the danger and misery you're trying to bring on yourself—" She told Sarah to put that bucket down and come inside the house.

When Mama and Sarah were gone, Amy gave William a sarcastic look and he picked up a clod and threw it directly between her shoulders. There would likely have been a fight after that except that they were too much interested in wondering what Mama was saying to scold Sarah.

Whatever it was, when Sarah came back she didn't have so much of the look in her eyes that William had noticed in her father's picture. And she didn't lift any more heavy buckets of cuttings during the week it took them to get their potato crop started.

Nugget followed every move they made while they worked in the garden, sometimes at Sarah's heels, just as often at William's or Amy's. Lots of times Sarah would stop work and gather the puppy up in her arms, cuddling it against her cheek, letting it curl up close to her neck. William watched her at such times, greatly pleased. "You sure like her, don't you, Sarah?" he asked her once.

"Whatever makes you think that, William? Can't you see that I don't care a rap about the silly little thing?" she said, putting on a big pretend-act. When she said that, Sarah looked over at Amy and laughed—but Amy had a hard time behaving toward Sarah the way Mama said she should. She didn't return Sarah's laughing look, just remarked to no one in particular that Nugget wasn't nearly so cute as Duchess had been when she was a puppy.

Sarah acted as if she hadn't heard Amy's words or didn't care much about them anyway, but William was mad. It was spitey-cat meanness in Amy, he thought, but he didn't say anything.

Amy got down from her high horse though a few days later. She was used to making good grades in school, and Mama was always glad when either Amy or William brought home a good report card. But a new math teacher had come into school at midyear and he wasn't explaining Amy's algebra lessons so that she could understand them. Sometimes Amy studied and studied and then went to her room bawling and that made Mama feel bad because she didn't know how to help Amy with new math. When Mama was in school, kids still studied old math, and Mama was glad that William got his problems done without any trouble because she wasn't sure that she understood even his fourth-grade math well enough to be much help. Anyway, sometimes she had to stay in her room and didn't even notice when Amy was upset over algebra.

Then one night when Mama told Sarah about Amy's trouble with math. Sarah offered to help. She had studied lots of algebra the new math way in high school, and that night she sat at the table with Amy and explained things so that Amy understood them better than she ever had before. Well, William was glad to see that Amy showed she'd had a decent bringing up. Just as ladylike as you please, she said, "Thank you, Sarah, I can't tell you how much I appreciate your help." And later on she picked Nugget up, telling her that she was a sweet thing—more like Duchess every day she got older.

When Amy was gone, Sarah patted Nugget and grinned at William. "This puppy will never know what it owes to new math," she said, and William got the gist of what she meant. She was laughing at Amy, but not mad at her. He shook his head without saying anything; he was on Sarah's side, he thought, but he didn't want to make fun of his sister if that's what Sarah's words were doing.

Sarah would work, maybe all morning in the garden, then she'd go to one of the cool rooms on the north side of Mary Hand's house or sometimes under the shade trees on the lawn and there she'd put up her easel and paint. She painted all kinds of things—pictures of Carla, some of Nugget, one of a small lizard perched upon a rock and looking for all the world, Sarah said, like a saucy little piece of sculpture. Once she made a sketch of Mary Hand's house with the bright flowering bushes all around it—everywhere touched with sunlight. When the sketch was finished she packed it carefully in a flat package with cardboard on either side and asked William to take it to the post office on his way to school.

"I'll bet Mary Hand will be happy when she sees that," William guessed, and Sarah said yes, she thought so.

Sometimes she let William stand behind her and watch a picture slowly come to life under her brushes. "It's like you know some kind of magic, Sarah," he told her one day.

She glanced up to give him just a friendly smile at first, but then her face grew thoughtful and a little frown came between her brows. "Let me look at your eyes, William," she said—that was all, but she looked and looked at him with that level gaze of hers that seemed to go right down to rock bottom. Then she had him turn around and she stood off a little distance, making her eyes narrow as she studied him. William didn't understand what she was up to.

"I'm going to paint a Sweet William picture," she said after a while. "I'm going to do an oil of my friend William Morrison Saunders—if I can only get those eyes right."

He was pleased but he felt apologetic. "I'm not pretty like Amy," he reminded her.

"You're my kind of pretty," she answered, and right away she began making sketches of him—his mouth, his nose, and page after page with nothing on them except a pair of brown eyes.

She worked from time to time for many days, sometimes turning his face this way and that, often looking at him so long and soberly that he'd crack up with giggles. Then she'd send him away.

"Shove off," she'd say, "and come back when you can keep your face straight." He didn't always want to leave, but he knew enough to get going when Sarah spoke in that tone.

Finally one day she laid her brushes aside and motioned him to come and stand beside her. She pointed to the picture, smiling at the corners of her mouth, and William looked at it with wonder.

A little boy holding a golden puppy in his arms stood there among the colors Sarah had splashed on her canvas to give the idea of flowers without really painting them. The boy had a smooth, slender face and big eyes that had kind of a sadness in them, although his mouth seemed ready to break into a smile at any minute. He wore faded old work-clothes and his feet were bare in the grass. You'd have thought that maybe this kid was just through picking oranges or hoeing potatoes and had come in to have a romp with his puppy.

They found a frame in the attic, and when the picture was all ready they took it over to William's house.

"This is for you, Mama," Sarah said. Mama cried, but she liked it a lot. She asked them to hang it on the wall opposite her bed and sometimes William would come in to find her looking at the painting and smiling to herself.

By the time strawberries were ripe in mid-April Sarah no longer looked slim and little as she had the first night he talked to her in Mary Hand's yard. He knew what it meant—the baby inside her was growing big; he wondered sadly if a man and woman down in Miami were counting the weeks until they'd have Sarah's baby for their own.

But in spite of her heaviness, Sarah wanted to go with Amy and William to Mr. Cooper's strawberry field where he allowed people to pick berries for only a few cents a quart. And so they went out one day. Amy had to stay with Mama, but Sarah and William each took a basket and walked across the field with Carla between them holding on to their hands and with Nugget frisking ahead of them, going a bit crazy at being allowed to be one of the party.

They picked berries all morning, paying no attention to the hot sun or the insects that came along to settle on their sweaty faces. Every now and then either William or Sarah would guide Carla's hand into a thick clump of berries, and she was proud as she held out handfuls of ripe fruit to drop into the baskets they moved toward her. Finally when the heat grew too intense, they set her under a shade tree to rest and play with Nugget while they finished their morning's work.

After a while—when weariness had kept them silent for a long time—Sarah stopped working and began telling William something it seemed she'd been thinking about.

"Strawberries always remind me of a time at my grandmother's out in the country when I was little," she said, and William stopped work too, eager to hear a story. "We had gone there from our apartment in New York because my father had been very ill. I remember that one morning I went out by myself and filled a tin pail with wild strawberries I found along a fence-row. They weren't anywhere nearly as big as these, but they were ripe and sweet. I only ate two or three of them because I was so anxious to fill a bowl and carry them out to the porch where my father was sitting in the sun. When my grandmother saw me taking them out to him, she said, 'Well Jason, you surely have a little girl who loves you.' He cried when she said that—I didn't know why at the time—"

"Do you know now?" William asked when she paused.

"I think so. I think he knew that he was going to leave me and go back to New York alone. And he knew that was going to break both our hearts."

She didn't say anything more for a while and William waited, hating to question her but wanting very much to know what happened. Finally he asked timidly, "And did he leave you, Sarah?"

She shook her head. "No, I saw to that. When his car pulled out one morning and I realized he was going to leave without me, I ran after him screaming at the top of my lungs. He kept leaning out, telling me to go back, and I kept on running and screaming. I think I would have run until I died if he hadn't stopped."

"Did he spank you?" William asked, almost afraid to hear what happened.

"No. Jason never spanked me in all my life—not even when some people thought I needed spanking. He just picked me up in his arms that day and said yes, we'd go back to our dumpy little apartment and be happy together—"

William suddenly noticed that there were tears on Sarah's cheeks. He was surprised. Somehow she had seemed like a girl who would never cry.

After a while William said, "That's the way Mama feels. She keeps telling us that staying together is important—"

"It is," Sarah said soberly. "It's *very* important."

Mama had said they should pay Mr. Cooper the few cents for each quart of berries that other pickers were paying him. But when they stopped at the fruit stand, Mr. Cooper said no, that if Sarah would freeze some berries and make jam for herself and the other three kids, he guessed he could furnish the strawberries.

That afternoon while Mama slept, Sarah and Amy made strawberry jam and filled bags of berries for freezing. The two girls worked together, friendlier that afternoon than they ever had been before, while William filled bowls with the firmest berries—a bowl for each of them including Sarah, who would be staying for supper that evening. If only Mama could have stayed comfortable all evening, it would have been almost like a party.

All spring the garden grew, sometimes stunted for a while by drought, then blossoming out green and sturdy when the rains finally came. All during late spring and early summer they ate from the garden, buying as little meat as possible, having a treat of baked fish every three or four weeks when Robert Norris came back from a fishing trip and brought a fine big red snapper especially for Mama. Sometimes he'd go back out to his truck and bring in his guitar because he knew that Mama liked to hear him play. Sarah liked it too, and she and William and Carla would sing with Robert, sometimes for a whole evening. Amy never wanted to sing with them; usually she pretended that she had to study and went off to her room.

I don't get it, William thought. I know she *likes* Robert, but then it would take a Philadelphia lawyer—as Mr. Cooper always said—to understand Amy.

As the weeks went by Sarah gradually began to take over the cooking and to have her meals with William and his family. She had a way of cooking that Amy hadn't yet learned. She would cook some little onions and Mexican peppers and zucchini, season it all with the garlic butter she'd fixed earlier and kept wrapped in the refrigerator. Once in a while one of Mrs. Cooper's friends who worked in a supermarket in town brought out some cheese for both Mrs. Cooper and Mama. She said the manager of the market threw cheese away if it collected

43

mold because she said people wouldn't buy it. Sarah said good heavens, cheese was made from mold and she would trim it with a few quick slashes of Mama's paring knife and add it to her skillet of good things. It made a dish you'd pay plenty for at a restaurant in town.

"How did you learn to cook things the way you do, Sarah?" Amy asked one day, and Sarah answered, "My father was a good cook, and he let me help him. He used to say that he had more talent with a skillet than a paintbrush. That wasn't quite true, but he did have a feeling for herbs and sauces and the way certain vegetables blend with others."

Once when Sarah made a pot of soup with all the vegetables she could find cooked with the stock made from a meat-bone, Mama said, "It smells so good, Sarah; maybe I could eat a bowl of it."

William knew it was a good sign if Mama felt like eating and he hardly breathed as he watched her lift the first spoonfuls of the soup to her mouth. But his hopes didn't last long. Mama tried her best—he knew she did—but after a minute she shook her head and laid her spoon aside.

She lived mostly on ginger ale these days, but one afternoon Sarah bought ice cream and Mama was able to eat a small dish of it. After that, Sarah and Amy saw to it that there was ice cream in the refrigerator all the time. Mama seemed to enjoy the cool sweetness, but she was always worried. "Have you put some of this aside for Carla?" she would ask each time one of the girls served a dish of ice cream to her. After several weeks Amy and Sarah often asked William to take Carla over to Mary Hand's house and read to her or play little games. Sarah found some clay on one of her trips into town to buy art supplies and she showed William how to help Carla mold animal figures out of the clay—an elephant with a great trunk, a giraffe with a long neck, a lion with a ruffled mane around its head. Carla's fingers soon found the clues which allowed her to recognize each animal, and she would work for hours, talking to her clay lions and giraffes, making them dash through an imaginary forest, having them tell her stories about their little children who were learning to read Braille out in Pine Woods. Carla was pleased to go over to Mary Hand's house with William, to sing at the top of her voice, and to listen to the scratchy old records on Mary's phonograph. The girls were right, William thought; it was much better for Carla to be away when Mama's pain was hurting her most.

He thought often about Sarah's baby as he sat alone with Carla, wondering what would become of it, hoping that maybe Sarah would change her mind about giving it away, but feeling a kind of aching sureness that she wouldn't. Sarah was not a girl who changed her mind once she had decided on something.

One morning when Mama was feeling better, William sat beside her bed and they talked quietly together about the garden, about the letter from a man who had taken one of Duchess's puppies and had written to tell them what a fine young animal it was getting to be. The subject of Duchess's puppies made William remember things Sarah had said the night he took Nugget over to her.

"Do you think we'll get to see the baby, Mama?" he asked, trying to believe that Mama would say yes, that she thought Sarah might change her mind about giving it away.

But she didn't. "It's due in early August, but you must put your hopes down, William. We won't ever get to see it—"

"The people in Miami, I guess?" he questioned.

"Yes. Dr. Finley says they're very anxious to adopt it."

"And Sarah won't even look at it?"

"She thinks it's better for the baby if she knows nothing about it—how big it is, whether it's a girl or a boy, the name of the people who are adopting it—"

"Do *you* think that's right, Mama?"

She stroked his hand several times before she answered. Then she said, "Who can say, William? A baby needs a home with a father and mother—"

"We don't have a father any more and we're managing because we've got you—"

"Yes. But Sarah is very young. It might be hard for a girl like her to raise a child alone and make a living. Sarah has no relatives closer than Mary Hand, and she's a very distant relative—getting old, too—"

"She has us. I'd work hard to help feed that baby—"

Mama smiled. "I know you would. But it's Sarah's decision, honey, and we're not wise enough to know exactly what's best." She held his hand up to her lips. "Try not to worry, William; try to think of other things."

"Yes, ma'am," he said. He realized there were a lot of things to think about that summer.

four

LATE IN July Mr. Cooper stopped at the house one day to tell Mama about a hurricane that was building up hundreds of miles south in the Caribbean Sea. Sarah had been listening to the news about the storm and she and William had located the Caribbean Sea on a map in one of Mary Hand's books and had found the islands that the people at the weather bureau said were being "buffeted by winds up to a hundred miles an hour."

"We won't worry Mama about this," Sarah said, but Mr. Cooper thought it best to warn her.

"That old tropical devil is driftin' to the northwest," he told Sarah. "It just might mean trouble for folks in these parts."

Mama no longer read the morning paper as she used to do and Papa's old radio in her room hadn't been turned on in many months. When the hurting was bad, she had no wish to listen to it; when the medicine made her more comfortable she could only think of going to sleep and being free of pain. After hearing about the hurricane, however, she turned on the radio and sometimes she looked at Amy and William fearfully as she listened.

"We were struck once—up in South Carolina when I was a child," she said. She shook her head though, and refused to say anything more when William asked her what a hurricane was like.

"I know they're sayin' there's a possibility of the storm strikin' our side of the state," Mr. Cooper said, "but it's only one chance in ten or fifteen—maybe more." He looked at Mama and anyone could see that he was worried, though he tried to talk brave.

"Now don't let it fret you, Libby. These storms veer and twist 'til you'd think they'd be dizzy—which I guess maybe they are. I've knowed 'em to look like they're headin' straight for this old pine woods and then have a change of mind and hightail it off into the Gulf. This storm, like as not, will never touch us."

But in a day or two the news sounded more and more fearful. Mr. Cooper's big red face, usually so full of smiles when he dropped in to say hello, was very sober. When the newscasts began to sound worse he brought a big roll of wide tape which he handed to William.

"Not that I think this storm is goin' to hit us," he said, "but just to be on the safe side, you and Amy might put strips of this across your windows." He showed them how to do it, and then he went with William across to Mary Hand's house and showed Sarah how to make the windows safer over there. He found a pile of thin slats stored under the back porch, and told Sarah to nail them across the big window in front and the glass door that opened out on the north porch.

"Bring in all the chairs and flowerpots from the porch," he told her. "Get plenty of grub in for Libby's family and for yourself. If things begin to look bad, draw kettles of water—fill the bathtubs with water over here and over at Libby's too. I don't want to worry her with more than I have to—you'll see after things for her, won't you?"

"Yes," Sarah said. She looked at William with worry in her eyes.

They worked hard all the next day and stopped only to hear the latest news from the weather bureau. Mr. Cooper told Mama that she and the kids could come over to his house if the storm got bad; but she said no, she'd just as well stay and face it in her own home. Mr. Cooper said she was right—that one place was just about as safe as another.

William helped Sarah and Amy carry some of the things Mama valued most up to the attic in case of flooding. There was the little sewing cabinet Papa had made for her when they were first married; there was the painting Sarah had done of William, and albums full of snapshots taken of Amy and William and Carla from the time they were babies. They put bedding and clothes up on the highest closet shelves and made a bed for Duchess in the kitchen so she wouldn't have to be outside. Mama told the girls where to find candles and medicines and bandages in case of hurts made by falling glass.

Mary Hand's house was on a little knoll—there wasn't quite so much danger of flooding over there; still, William and Sarah carried everything they could manage up to the second floor. All but Sarah's bed—she wanted her bed and Nugget's left in the kitchen where she felt closer to Mama and the kids next door.

By the end of the week the people at the weather bureau sounded excited and scared, and the sky looked excited and scared too. The high winds sent clouds of a dirty, yellowish color scudding across the sky and the air was heavy, hard to breathe.

William went into town with Amy on Friday morning to buy groceries that Sarah thought they might need. Everybody in the stores talked hurricane, and some of the stories they told about hurricanes of other years sent cold waves along William's spine. He pulled at Amy's hand when she seemed to forget everything while she listened to the horror stories, and after a minute they began loading things into the little express wagon and started for home.

They had bought everything that Sarah had written on her list: powdered milk, peanut butter, oatmeal, dry beans, plenty of ginger ale for Mama and a quart of the ice cream she liked to eat. Sarah asked Amy to pick out a plump chicken for roasting that night. "I'll cook a party supper and we'll enjoy it while we listen to the hurricane roar," she said lightly, but William wasn't fooled. He knew that Sarah was as scared as he and Amy were.

Mama had said no, that Sarah mustn't make the long trip into town and back with Amy and William that morning, and so Sarah stayed at home to look after Carla and to nail more slats across some of the windows that were still unprotected. It was a good thing she hadn't gone with them—William thought as he trudged along pulling the wagon-load of groceries—because by the time they left town, the going was beginning to get rough. Damp wind picked up sand from the road and blew grains of it into their faces where it stung as if it was a hundred tiny needles cutting into their flesh. They were panting when they finally got home; William felt his lungs ache as if dust and strange gases were getting into them with the stormy air. Sarah heated soup for them as soon as they came inside and hunted up cold cream for them to rub on their faces. Carla was asleep, she told them, after a restless morning, and Mama lay, peaceful for a time, in her bedroom. They were all tired and Amy said that Sarah had better go over to Mary Hand's house and get some rest while she and William took naps in their rooms.

As she started out across the two yards, Sarah turned to William. "If I should oversleep, come and wake me in time to cook our chicken for supper." William nodded. He was not likely to forget that.

It grew dark by late afternoon, when the July sun should still have been well up in the sky. It was a thick darkness with something mean in it. The wind kept getting stronger and the big palms in the dooryard bent and swayed whenever a hard gust hit them. Out in the pine woods there was a great threshing of branches, one on the other, and the whole woods sounded troubled. William went out to his thinking stone and stood for a while, his face lifted to the sky.

About five o'clock the rain began to come down in earnest. The radio was dead, but Mama didn't need the man from the weather bureau to tell her what was happening. "Hurricane rain," she said, and her eyes grew wide as she looked out the window. William stood at her side and they watched the great sheets of rain sweep down and slap the walls of their little house.

Finally Mama turned to him. "I think you'd better go tell Sarah to come over before this gets any worse. Tell her to plan on staying over here with us tonight."

William drew a raincoat over his head and around his shoulders before he ran out into the downpour. He had a glimpse of the Gulf, far out beyond the woods, where the white waves were beginning to leap into the air. He whistled for Duchess to go with him, but she whined and cowered inside the kitchen door. "Just as you please, girl," he called to her, "but if you stay inside 'til this is over you're goin' to be housebound for a while."

As he ran into the storm he began to feel more and more excited and eager. He spread his arms wide and dared the wind-driven rain to make him afraid. He yelled and raced out to the woods where he climbed on top of his thinking stone and laughed at the tumult around him. "Come on, hurricane," he shouted, "how about a little action?"

There were no lights in Mary Hand's house and William thought sure enough, that Sarah was oversleeping as she had been afraid she might do. He ran up the steps to the back porch and knocked at the kitchen door before he turned the knob.

Inside, he found Sarah seated on the edge of her cot, bent almost double with Nugget whimpering at her feet. She was breathing in little gasps and once she pressed her arms against her swollen middle as if she seemed to be fighting back something hurtful that was happening to her.

"What's the matter, Sarah?" William asked, scared— all the excitement of a moment before completely gone. "Aren't you going to come over and cook the party supper for us like you said?"

"I won't be able to cook supper tonight, William. I think the baby is going to be born—"

She looked at him with so much trouble in her eyes that William ran in panic toward the door, but he stopped when she called to him. "Call the Coopers, William; maybe they will come over and drive me to the hospital."

He hurried to the telephone, but when he lifted the receiver there was no dial tone. Complete silence. "The line is dead, Sarah," he panted, and Sarah gave a little moan.

It was hard for William to pull the kitchen door open against the force of the wind when he got home. Mama was sitting in the living room with Carla in her lap. When William told her about Sarah she sat staring at him without answering.

"I can't," she said finally in a crying whisper. "I can't go through with it. I don't have the strength—" She raised her eyes to look at Amy's scared face, at William drenched with hurricane rain. "I can't do it," she said; and Amy answered no, Mama couldn't, that Sarah had no right to expect someone as sick as Mama to help her have a baby.

Mama stared out the window for a minute without saying anything more, then she suddenly put Carla down and got to her feet. "Wrap Carla in my raincoat, Amy; you'll have to carry her. William, fill a bag with all the groceries you can pack in it and the candles from the top drawer of my dresser. I'll get our clothes together, and when you've carried Carla and the groceries over, come back for me. Don't cry, Carla, everything's going to be all right. Amy will get you ready for bed just as soon as she and William have helped Mama over to Sarah's—"

Neither William nor Amy ever argued with Mama when she spoke in a tone like that. They got Carla ready and carried her over, intending to take her upstairs as Mama told them to do, but Carla was frightened and began to scream as she used to do when they first left her at the school for the blind.

Amy stopped at the kitchen door with Carla in her arms. "Can you calm her a little, Sarah? Mama will be here as soon as William and I can get back to help her."

Sarah held out her arms to Carla and the little girl clung to her, growing quieter as Sarah spoke in a low voice to her. William was glad—if you could call it glad when there was trouble everywhere. A wonder flashed through his mind about what had become of that boy who had felt brave enough to laugh at the storm only a few minutes ago. He took a long breath and then he and Amy started back to get Mama.

They found her holding Duchess's leash and wearing Papa's old raincoat, which covered her from head to foot. She carried a bag of hastily prepared sandwiches which would serve as supper; from a pocket in her coat she took a bottle containing the pills Dr. Finley gave her and held it out to William. "Take care of these, William," she told him, "they'll have to help me through this night."

They would have read stories to Carla in the bedroom

upstairs until she got over her fear, but seconds after Amy flipped the light switch, the electricity went off leaving the room in darkness. Then a din broke out in the dooryard that was even louder than the roar of the wind. Live wires broken between supporting poles began coiling and thrusting, spitting and bellowing with a fury that numbed William—as well as Amy and Carla—with fear. Then as suddenly as they had erupted, the wires lost their fire and were silent. "Maybe someone has turned off the power in town," William whispered, "or the wind has ripped the wires off the poles." Amy sobbed uncontrollably for a minute and then lifted Carla in her arms and tried to comfort her.

They were able to calm Carla's terror after a while, in spite of their own. They put night clothing on her and coaxed her to eat part of a sandwich. Then as her weariness grew and the roar of the wind became monotonous, she was able to sleep.

William and Amy changed from their drenched clothing to warm pajamas and then stood side by side at the window, unable to see much except sheets of swirling rain, but unwilling to turn back to the blackness of the room. Amy put her arm around William's shoulder and he felt the sort of kindness toward her that Mama often talked about when she hoped he and Amy would soon be too grown-up for quarreling and yelling at one another.

The wind grew fiercer as the hours passed; out in the pine woods they heard trees crash as if some giant might be out there cutting a pile of kindling for his fire. Closer to them, the biggest palm in Mary Hand's yard came crashing against the house, tearing away the screened walls of the north porch. They heard wood splinter and even the taped panels in the door crackled with the sound of broken glass.

A while later there was a great crashing and tearing of wood over at their own house. In the continuous lightning flashes, they could see their kitchen roof ripped off and hurled across the vegetable garden. Amy gasped. "What's to become of us, William?" she whispered fearfully when she was able to speak, and, of course, there wasn't any answer he could give her.

Then Mama came upstairs through the darkness. "Did you see it, Mama? Did you see what happened to our roof?" Amy asked.

"Yes, Amy, at least I heard it." Mama put her arms around both of them and they all stood close together in the darkness listening to the roar and the crashes outside. Finally Mama said, "I wish I could tell you not to be afraid, but of course you are. This is a fearful night for all of us. We'll just have to hold firm—maybe it will pass—" She stopped speaking, but her arms tightened around them and her closeness was better than any words.

"Is the baby born, Mama?" Amy asked after a while.

Mama's sigh seemed to come from the deepest part of her. "Not yet," she said, "not for a few more hours, I'm afraid."

When she had gone back downstairs, William turned to his sister. "Do you know what having a baby is like, Amy?" he asked.

Amy shook her head. "Just that it hurts," she answered.

"Do people ever die when they have babies?"

"Yes. Mr. and Mrs. Cooper's oldest girl died having a baby a long time ago—years before I was born—" Then to William's surprise she added, "Poor little Sarah—I hope she's all right."

The roar outside went on. Once some bricks were blown from one of the chimneys, falling like heavy hailstones on the roof, rattling the windows and shaking the rooms upstairs until a hanging lamp out in the hall swayed and crashed against the ceiling. It was a frightening sound, but after that last punishment dealt out to the old house, there was a pause as if the winds couldn't for that moment find anything more to smash or tear.

William stood unmoving at the window. Now and again he told himself, She won't die. She'll fight hard—she won't let the hurt kill her. But those were only words. He couldn't be sure that they meant anything, and his dread for Sarah became harder for him to bear than his fear of the wildness outside.

As the night went on, they were too tired to stand at the window any longer. Amy went to sleep beside Carla, and William stretched out on the floor beside their bed. He could have found a bed in one of the other rooms, but he wanted to be near Amy and Carla that night.

At dawn the girls were still asleep when William got to his feet and looked out of the window again. Morning was hardly more than a murky grayness coming through the rain which still poured but was not driven by the high winds that had whipped it a few hours earlier. Dimly he could see forms of uprooted trees, of telephone poles leaning over as if about to topple at any minute. The yard was like a lake and he could hear water lapping at the steps that led up to the front entrance. He felt despair as he guessed how high the water must be on the lower ground around his own home.

He opened the door and listened. There wasn't a sound from downstairs, and he wondered if he dared to go down and talk to Mama and Sarah. He was afraid though. There had been a reason why Mama's voice had been sharp when she said that he and Amy were to stay upstairs with Carla until she gave them permission to come down.

He waited for several minutes. There was no sound and finally he dared to speak. "Mama?" he called in a low voice.

It was Sarah who answered him. "Mama's asleep, William, but it's all right. You can come down."

He hurried down the steps, through the living room, down the hall to the dining room and then to the kitchen. The hurricane dawn made the room more like shadowy night than morning, but he could see Mama lying on a bed made atop two chairs which were drawn up close to Sarah's bed. She lay on her back with her hands across her midriff as if even in sleep she must press back against the pain in this part of her body. Sarah's hand was stretched out and it touched Mama's shoulder.

"She's in deep sleep," Sarah said. "She took the last pill before it was time for her to have it. She had to do it though; the pain was so bad—"

Sarah's face was as white as the chalk in school and there was no good-morning smile for William such as he was used to seeing there. Her big eyes had a tired look in them. He turned away from Sarah quickly and moved closer to the makeshift bed where his mother lay. A sharp fear went through him—she was so still, terribly still—and at first he was terrified, believing that Sarah was holding back word of some awful thing that had happened to Mama. Then he saw his mother's thin blouse rise and fall gently with her breathing, and he put his hand on her forehead with a sigh of relief.

He stood there for a long time, looking down at Mama. The wind—maybe because it was tired of its long hours of howling—had grown calm, though the rain kept on beating at the windows as if it had no thought of stopping. After a while he looked up to see Sarah watching him.

He was afraid at first to ask the question that was on his mind. Finally though, he spoke very cautiously. "Is there a baby, Sarah?"

"Yes," she said barely loud enough for him to hear. Then she pointed to a tiny mound under the blanket at her side. "Here's the baby. A little girl."

William lifted a corner of the blanket and stared at the small creature, fascinated. He had been too young when Carla was born to remember how she looked, and he had never seen so young a baby since. She was a splotchy red color, bald, with thick gold lashes touching her cheeks as she slept. Her mouth was puckered up in the middle of her face, a small O or possibly a small pink flower.

For a few minutes William forgot the beating rain and Mama's deep sleep and the tired look in Sarah's eyes. His voice came out glad and eager. "Can we keep her, Sarah? Please, can we keep her?"

"Yes, we'll keep her," Sarah answered, "I'm not sure that we're doing her a big favor—but we'll keep her."

"Yes, we *are* doing her a big favor—I know we are, Sarah." Then at a sudden thought he said, "You had to look at her, didn't you?"

She smiled, just barely. "Yes, I had to look at her. And give her an early breakfast—that was my undoing."

"Now you're glad, aren't you, that the hurricane wouldn't let you get to the hospital and give her away?"

Sarah drew the baby closer to her. "I'm glad we have her here, safe and healthy. I'm not so sure that I can thank the hurricane for much—" She shuddered as she spoke. "Is anything besides this house left standing?"

He told her about their roof and the big palm crashing into the north window of Mary Hand's living room; he told her about the bricks blown from the chimneys. Then he walked to the window and reported all he could see as the morning grew a little lighter. "Our yards look like lakes, Sarah—and so does Mr. Cooper's truck patch—and the trees have telephone wires and power lines hanging from their tops down into the water. Oh boy, are we going to have a mess to clean up around here—" The mess *was* great, but the long night of shrieking wind and fear was over. More than that they had a baby they were going to keep. William's voice grew cheerful as he spoke.

But Sarah was not cheerful. She closed her eyes at his words and turned her head on the pillow. After a while she reached out and took his hand.

"Mama left a flame on an old oil laundry stove in the storeroom when she made coffee at three this morning. Do you think, William, that you could cook a kettle of oatmeal? All of you must be hungry—and I have to think about regaining my strength if we're to clean up after this storm—"

"I can do it, Sarah—I've made oatmeal for Carla lots of times when Mama wasn't able." He ran to get things together for oatmeal porridge, glad that he could do something for Sarah, doubly glad that she had asked him instead of waiting for Amy to come downstairs.

He had never been in the storage room before. It was a small dingy place filled with cast-off dishes, glass fruit jars, old electric toasters, and frying pans probably no longer any good but hoarded there instead of being thrown on a junk pile. The room was filled with a damp darkness and the musty smell of long unused places. William felt uneasy there for a while—the room was like some he'd seen in horror movies—but he was interested in doing a good job on the task Sarah had set for him and so he began to whistle and if there were any bats or vampires around, they stayed well hidden.

The laundry stove—which he guessed had not been

used in years until last night—was still lighted and he had only to remove the coffeepot from the flame and start his kettle of water heating. He measured out oatmeal as Mama had taught him to do and he got salt and butter from the kitchen for seasoning.

Duchess and Nugget, hungry and upset at being shut up in the crowded storeroom all night, nudged his legs and he went to find food for them while the water heated. The rain still splashed against the windows and, when he opened the back door a crack, a wet sheet swept inside as if it had been waiting for the chance.

Suddenly Sarah's baby began to cry—shrill piercing wails that you wouldn't expect from so tiny a child—then stopped as suddenly as she had begun. Fearful that something was wrong, William ran up to the kitchen and over to Sarah's bed. Her eyes were closed as if they were heavy with sleep and the baby was tugging at her breast, the way Duchess's puppies had tugged at their mother months ago.

As William stood looking at Sarah, he felt a kind of sadness and happiness mixed up together. This baby made Sarah different from the girl she'd been before; once he had asked his mother "Would you say she's mostly kid or mostly grown-up?" There was no doubt now. She was mostly grown-up.

Getting food from the refrigerator for the dogs, William hurried back to feed them and then stood beside the stove watching a thin cloud of steam rise in the air. After the excitement of seeing the baby, of looking at the wreckage left by the hurricane outside, he was beginning to feel very tired from too few hours of sleep. Things seemed unreal and strange—all at once he was in a different world from the one he'd known yesterday morning. He hadn't wakened in his own home, and if he had, he would probably have found himself in a room half-full of water. The familiar countryside was gone; in its place was just water full of branches of trees and spikes from the picket fence—all kinds of litter that the hurricane had made and thrown aside. And now there was a baby to be cared for, and there was Sarah, no longer the girl he had known, but a grown-up woman, tired and worried like Mama.

The newness of things made him shiver once; then he turned determinedly to pour oatmeal into the kettle before him. Everything, he thought, would seem better when they'd all had a hot breakfast. What everyone needed was plenty of rest and good hot oatmeal. Then maybe the world would seem more like it had been before the hurricane.

five

It took days and weeks to clear away the mess left by the hurricane and to repair the damage done by it. Oranges, still green, but large as baseballs, had been stripped from the trees and lay rotting in the mud until Mr. Cooper came with his big shovels and scooped up the fruit Mama had counted on selling early in the winter. Mr. Cooper told William that, sad as it was to lose all their fruit crop, things could have been worse. He said that had the storm's eye hit them squarely, everything in the neighborhood would have been wiped out. Not only would the fruit have been stripped from the trees, but the trees themselves might have been torn out by their roots, leaving no chance of ever having a fruit crop again.

"I didn't know things could have been worse," William said, and he listened wide-eyed as he heard neighbors talk to Mr. Cooper about what would have happened if the Gulf had been at high tide instead of low when the storm struck, about the damage further upstate which was more terrible and frightening than anything people in the Pine Woods area had known.

Mr. Cooper scooped up piles of boards and poles and trees, the roof from the kitchen, loads of glass from broken windows, bricks from crumpled chimneys. Robert Norris came out from town and helped stretch a tarpaulin over the kitchen until such time when Mama could afford to have a carpenter come out and fix it right.

After the tarpaulin was in place, Robert Norris mended the chimneys and he told Sarah who to call about replacing the glass door that had been smashed by the falling palm tree.

Mama was glad to see Robert. She kissed him like he was her own boy, and he put his arms around her, gentle and nice, the way he always treated her. Amy acted the way she'd been acting toward him lately, not exactly mean but not friendly either. William had an idea it was because she wished Robert was her boyfriend and didn't want him to know it. Many a time William had heard Mary Hand tell how when Amy was a little kid they'd all laughed because she'd tell everyone who would listen that she was going to marry Robert. Amy'd started that because Robert used to bring her toys from the dime store and carry her piggyback around the yard when he came out with his father to help Papa pick the oranges. And only last year when Amy was twelve, she'd cried hard one day after Robert brought out a girl he was dating and acted like he thought the girl was really something. William had tried to tease Amy about that crying spell, but Mama brought him up short.

"That's a cruel thing to do, William," Mama had said. William stopped teasing, of course, but he couldn't see why it was cruel. Robert was eighteen then and getting ready to go to night school in a college. He was too old and too smart, William thought, for a kid like Amy. Maybe Amy thought so too; maybe that's why she acted so standoffish and never had a word to say when Robert was around.

Sarah asked Robert to stay for supper the night after he had worked so hard helping them clear up after the hurricane, and he was pleased. He listened to Carla sing some of her songs and promised her that he'd bring his guitar the next time he came out so that he could play music with her songs. He thought the baby was nice, and he told Sarah all about his work in night school which was going to help him be a landscape gardener some day. He would have told Amy about it too, but she acted like she wasn't listening.

Once he turned to Mama and said, "Libby, I think that by vacation time next spring William will be big enough to have a job helping me with the mowing and trimming on my work in town. Would that be all right with you?"

William felt proud when he heard that, and he could see that Mama was glad too. She said, "I'd feel happy to have him working with you, Robert."

After a few weeks Sarah was as strong as ever and she went with William and Amy over to the house that had been home to the Saunders all their lives. There, they worked until they ached at clearing piles of mud left on the floors when the water ran off, at ripping up carpets, at moving mattresses and bedding outside to dry in the sun and fresh air. The smell of mildew was everywhere until Robert brought out a hose that sent a powerful spray over walls and ceilings and floors. It helped, and the hot sun steaming in through the open windows helped too, but the nice smell of home as William remembered it was gone.

They named the baby "Elizabeth" for Mama. Elizabeth seemed to like her name, or maybe she just liked the sound of William's voice when he called her by that name. Anyway it wasn't long until she smiled at him. All of them, Mama and Sarah and even Amy, said that Elizabeth's first smile came when William crooned her name to her.

They took turns holding her. Mama did it best. She knew how to press Elizabeth's little belly and pat her back so that the baby burped in sharp explosions that tickled William and Carla.

"You should say 'Excuse me' when you make that

noise, Elizabeth," Carla would tell her sometimes, but Elizabeth would simply explode louder than ever and give Carla a don't-care look from her big eyes which were like Sarah's.

At first Mama held the baby for a while each day. She would smile at her and sometimes kiss the tiny feet that wouldn't stay under their blanket. But after a few weeks, when her eyes were strange and staring because of the pain, Mama had no wish to hold the baby. Once when William carried Elizabeth toward her, hoping the baby would cheer her, Mama said, "No, William—no, no. Take her away, honey—Mama's not able to find any joy in her today—"

When the bedding was dry over at the little house, Sarah and Amy folded it into big bundles and carried it up to one of the closets in Mary Hand's house. Then they began to bring over all the clothes that had been left there, Mama's dishes and sewing cabinet, the picture of William that Sarah had painted.

"Why are we taking everything over to Mary Hand's house?" William asked Amy. "Won't we come back here when the house is all dried out again?"

That was the day Amy cried harder than he had ever seen her cry. Finally she said, "Mama's going to die in a few weeks, William. Dr. Finley told Sarah. And Sarah says it's better for us to live over there with her if we don't have Mama—"

He told himself at least a hundred times that fall that Dr. Finley was wrong, that Mama was not going to die. Amy had said "a few weeks" and when, not only a few weeks passed, but five or six of them, he was more sure than ever. After a time or two, though, he wouldn't tell anyone how sure he was. He didn't want to see that sad, unbelieving way people looked at him when he dared to tell them that Dr. Finley was wrong.

The doctor gave Sarah stronger medicine that would help to ease Mama's pain. Most of the time it kept her asleep, but even in her sleep she made sounds that showed the pain was still inside her. After a while she didn't even speak when William stood beside her bed; she looked up at him as if he was a strange boy she had never seen before.

Amy and Sarah took turns sitting beside Mama's bed day after day, and at night Amy slept in the rocking chair beside Mama until midnight and then she called Sarah. They bathed Mama's face in cool water, sometimes her whole body when the sun's heat grew fiercest and came inside the usually cool rooms. Mama got so she didn't know either of them, but even then, she would reach up and run her hand across Amy's cheek or Sarah's. Sometimes she would say "Thank you, girl," and that would make them take a deep breath and stare at one another without speaking.

William looked after Carla and the dogs; he did all he could to take care of Elizabeth too, although he had to look for help from the two big girls in caring for this smallest one. All of them shared the cooking chores, but William volunteered to do the dishwashing alone. In the early evening the three of them sat beside Mama's bed together. They didn't talk much; often it seemed like they were not able to say a word. They were all friends though—and family—and that was good.

That fall Amy and William were back in school again, Carla could go back to her class for the blind later on, but the two older ones must keep up with their work at school. Sarah said wasn't that what Mama would want them to do and, of course, it was.

But one day in October they didn't go to school. Sarah came upstairs very early that morning and William heard her go to Amy's room first and then come to his. She stood just inside the door, looking at him, her face strange, not like Sarah's face at all. She said, "Mama died a little while ago, William. It's better. She doesn't feel the pain now—"

Then Sarah began to shake as if a coldness had come over her. She said, "I can't quite remember the things Dr. Finley said that I must do. Go down to the telephone, William, and call the Coopers. Ask them if they'll please come over here and help us—"

A rain came down steadily the day of Mama's funeral. It was a chilling rain, the kind that hurts people most when they are not used to chill. In spite of the rain, however, everybody from the neighborhood came and many from town. There was Mr. Hager, the lawyer who had given Mama a job typing his work as long as she was able; there was Robert Norris and his parents; there were some nurses from the hospital and Dr. Finley; there were some of Amy's and William's teachers, good Mr. and Mrs. Cooper, of course—all of them kind people—but William was glad when everyone was gone and he was alone again with Amy and Sarah and the little girls.

About dusk all of them took turns talking to Mary Hand who called them from Albany, New York. Mary Hand was sad because she hadn't been able to come down and see Mama before she died. She kept saying that they must all live together in her house and be good to one another and not fight. After the long telephone talk was over, they sat in the living room where Sarah had built a fire in the fireplace because the house seemed chilly. They didn't say much—just sat and thought and listened to the rain against the windows.

At bedtime Amy said, "Can I sleep in your room tonight, Sarah?" Her eyes were full of tears as she stood at the bottom of the stairs and looked back before she started up to put Carla to bed.

William had never been quite sure whether Sarah and Amy ~~liked~~ one another or not, but at that moment when Sarah walked over and took Amy's hand there didn't seem to be any doubt. Amy leaned her head on Sarah's shoulder and Sarah stroked her hair for a minute before she spoke.

"Of course you can sleep in my room, Amy," she said quietly. "We can put the two twin beds together and Carla can lie there with us. We can make a bed in the armchair for Elizabeth—" She stopped speaking and looked at William, who sat silent in his chair, making no move to go upstairs with them. "Why don't you take the room next to mine, William? You can leave the connecting door open and we can all talk together until we're sleepy—"

He had never been sharp with Sarah before, but he was that night. He said "No"—a very short no—and then he went up to the room at the end of the hall where he had been sleeping since the days following the hurricane. Once inside, he closed the door with a firmness that was almost a slam, feeling with a keen loneliness that he was an outsider in this family of girls. William didn't want to leave a door open so that he could talk to them—he hadn't the slightest wish to talk to them. He only wanted to be alone in his room where he could think about Mama and wish that he could die too.

He looked over at the dark house on the other side of the fence and watched the tarpaulin flap continuously in the rain at one corner of what was left of the kitchen roof. He wondered if Mama's ghost was over there somewhere in the empty rooms and he thought that if it was, he wouldn't be afraid to see it. He'd put his arms around the little ghost, and in the morning he'd wake up and hear Mama singing a Sweet William song close to his ear.

The wet darkness suddenly looked too big and lonely for a nine-year-old boy to bear. He put his head down on the windowsill and sobbed.

He didn't hear her coming down the hall, but all at once Sarah was there wearing an old robe of Mary Hand's that trailed along the floor. She didn't ask him any questions; she didn't even seem to notice that he was crying. She said, "Amy's feeling better—she's rocking Carla to sleep. I told her I'd be back after I'd talked for a while to you—" Then Sarah put her arm around his shoulders and led him toward the stairs. "Let's go down to the kitchen and heat some milk for a nightcap." She drew him close to her side and they walked down the long flight of steps together.

Sarah heated milk at the stove and, when it was ready, poured it into two cups and carried them into the living room. She drew the couch up in front of the fireplace where a bed of red coals still filled the room with rosy light; then, taking a blanket from the hall closet she wrapped it around William's shoulders and drew him down to the corner of the couch, where she seated herself among the cushions.

"Let's sip our milk together," she said quietly. "It's good for us." She laid her cheek against his forehead for a second and her touch was so like Mama's that one more sob burst from his throat in spite of his effort to hold it back. After that they sat looking at the coals that still glowed in the fireplace—both of them silent, thinking their own thoughts.

Finally Sarah spoke. She said, "This is the bitterest night, William. Gradually we'll be able to bear it a little better."

"I don't think it will ever be better."

"It will. I thought I couldn't live when my father died. But you see, I did—"

"You loved him a lot, didn't you?" He asked the question, trying for a minute to get away from his own pain.

"Yes, a lot. More than a lot. I guess all the love in me belonged to him in those days—"

"He never made you go back to your grandmother's?" he asked, remembering the story she had told him the day they picked strawberries.

"No, we lived together for the rest of his life." She smiled suddenly at her thoughts. "There were lots of good times. If we had money, the sky was the limit—it shouldn't have been, but it was. One summer he took me to France and Italy and we saw the most wonderful pictures that have ever been painted—places I still dream about sometimes. That was great, but when we were down on our luck the next winter, we'd still find things to do that were fun. I can remember a long walk with him through cold, blustery streets, then coming home nearly frozen and feeling so rich because our apartment was warm and smelled of the soup he'd left to simmer on the stove—"

William imagined he could see this handsome, smiling father of Sarah's, could picture all the fun they'd had together. But when Sarah spoke again, her voice showed she was no longer glad to remember.

"It wasn't always like that, William. Sometimes my father was so sick with drinking that he'd lie in bed for days and I could hardly get him to eat anything. Over and over he would promise me that he'd never let himself get that way again. Maybe he'd keep his promise for months, then something would happen and we'd have to go through the whole terrible time of sickness again—"

"Didn't it make you mad at him?"

"Yes, so mad that I hate to think of it now. I used to believe that he had lied to me deliberately, that I could never trust him again. I know now that it was a sickness in him; he tried but he couldn't overcome it—"

"I used to be mad at Mama sometimes when I was little because I thought she liked Amy better than me—"

"But she didn't, did she, William? I don't believe she *could* have loved anyone more than she loved you."

"If she had got well, there's not a thing she would ever do that would make me mad at her again. Not one thing," he added, choking once more.

"I know." When she spoke again, her voice sounded different, businesslike.

"We've got to begin making plans, William, we've got to think about what we're going to do in the months ahead—"

"I'm awful scared about one thing, Sarah—"

"Tell me what you're scared about."

He hesitated, hating the words. "Orphan places," he said finally.

There was a determined look on Sarah's face as she answered him. "There'll be no 'orphan places,' William. Amy and I promised Mama that. We'll be the two big sisters, you'll be the man of the family, and the three of us will look after the little sprouts. No orphan places for any of us—that's a promise."

He took a deep breath that came out trembling. "Do you think we can get along without Mama telling us how to do things?" he asked. "I don't think Amy could—and you're not really very old, are you?"

"Not very old, but I'm very stubborn, William. Mary

Hand can tell you that—and the ladies at the orphanage. Jason could have too, for that matter. I don't give up without an awful ruckus—"

He couldn't have believed that he would smile on a night like this, but he did. A very small smile at the fierceness of Sarah's voice. "Mama said Mr. Hager would look after us," he said after a moment.

"He will. He'll help Amy and me keep things in line. The first thing he's doing is to give me a job next week—"

"But who'll take care of Elizabeth if you work for Mr. Hager?" he asked quickly, his face full of concern.

"There's a Mrs. Collins in town who takes care of babies from time to time. Elizabeth will stay with her during the day and we'll bring her home with us at night—" She paused and wrinkled her forehead at a sudden thought. "I have to learn how to make a feeding formula for her right away. Our young lady must take her meals out of bottles from now on—"

"There's lot of things to think about, ain't there, Sarah?"

"Lots. The roof over at your house must be fixed as soon as we can afford it—dampness is ruining the whole place. Mr. Cooper says I must give citrus food to the orange trees right away—no fruit this year, but we must look forward to next. We must pay Carla's tuition right away—they tell me that Mama forgot it during these last months. And we really ought to get Duchess and Nugget fixed so there'll be no more puppies. Another important thing for me to learn from Mr. Hager is how I'm to keep accounts—I must account for all the money that comes in to you children from the government, from selling oranges or vegetables, from renting half of the acre around your house—we *will* have to rent it, won't we? A half-acre is all we can possibly take care of until you're older—" She shook her head and rubbed her free hand over her eyes. "Well, we'll just have to take one thing at a time. I know Amy will help me. She's learned a lot by taking so much responsibility lately—"

"I'm glad you and Amy like each other. At first I was afraid you wouldn't—"

"I know. We were a little strained when I first came here. But I know I can depend on her now—"

"You can depend on me, Sarah," he said earnestly, and at his words she looked down into his eyes and smiled.

"I have all kinds of faith in you, William. No one need ever tell me that William Saunders has let me down because I'll say to that person, 'Well that just proves how cock-eyed you can be.' "

He didn't answer and they sat quietly in the shadows that were growing darker as the coals in the fireplace lost more and more of their glow. His weariness and loneliness were beginning to be less hurtful as sleep moved in to take over. After a while Sarah spoke in the soft voice she used when she rocked Carla or Elizabeth at bedtime.

"Go to sleep, William," she said. "The sun's going to be out again in the morning. Things will be brighter—a little more bearable—"

He didn't know when she laid him down among the cushions and went back upstairs to comfort Amy. But in the morning when he awoke the sun *was* shining and though the hurt of losing Mama was still there, it was something he could face and then keep hidden.

six

THINGS SEEMED strange for many days; there was an emptiness in their lives that all of them felt—even little Carla. For weeks she refused to sing. "Songs make me think about Mama," she said quietly when Sarah asked her to sing one day. But she enjoyed wheeling Elizabeth up and down the long porch in an old carriage that Mrs. Cooper loaned them and when Dr. Finley had taught Sarah how to make a feeding formula, Carla was happy to hold the bottle to the baby's eager mouth. After a few weeks they finally heard her singing softly to Elizabeth as she rocked the littlest member of their family to sleep. William felt comforted as he listened. Carla's singing was like a slow return to other days.

It was hard to get used to being a family without Mama. Even in the last weeks of her sickness, Mama's presence had meant that the household had a head. It was not the same now. "Just being a bunch of kids living together—even if one of the kids is mostly grown-up—is a different kind of family," William mused. It was somehow flimsy, a shaky kind of family that could suddenly blow up and separate all of them as Duchess's puppies had been separated. That was something Mama had dreaded; it was a thought that sent a chill through William whenever it entered his mind.

The three oldest divided the chores among themselves, and things worked out pretty well. Sarah did the cooking and the laundry; Amy cleaned the house; she and William did the dishes; and all of them, under Mr. Cooper's directions, took care of the gardening. Odd jobs had to be taken over by whoever could do the taking; William, in thinking it over, realized that it was usually Sarah who did the extras—Sarah who was older, a bit more like Mama.

When Mr. Hager gave Sarah a job in his office, all of them walked to town together very early each morning unless a rainstorm sent Mr. Cooper or some other neighbor to their rescue in covered trucks. They could have taken the road a half-mile north and boarded a bus into town, but the weekly expense of bus riding was too much. They could buy milk and cereal with what they saved by walking to town, on their own good legs, Sarah said; and William and Amy who had trudged the four-mile round trip daily for years, never gave a thought to the neighboring bus line.

William drew Carla, as he had for the past two years, in the little express wagon; Sarah bought an arm cradle for Elizabeth and they laid cradle and baby across Carla's lap. Then while William or Amy pulled the wagon, Sarah walked beside it, shielding Carla and Elizabeth from the blazing sun with an old purple umbrella they found in one of the upstairs closets.

They looked funny as they walked into town, William supposed after he heard some high school kids making fun of them. Amy heard it too, and she cried that night and got sullen so that the next day Sarah said why didn't Amy go on a half-hour earlier because she needed a study-period before class anyway.

"Why does she have to get so uptight about a bunch of dumb kids laughing at us?" William asked as they walked along that morning.

"Well, I suppose we do look a shade on the odd side, William," Sarah answered, pulling one of Mary Hand's old straw hats further down on her forehead, "and adolescents are shy about looking different—"

"What are 'adolescents'?" He didn't care particularly except that the word was big and sounded interesting.

"Persons in their teen years." Sarah juggled the umbrella so as to get both children in its shade.

"Then ain't you one of them?"

"Matter of fact, I believe I am. It hadn't occurred to me lately."

"Are *you* shy about being different?"

"No, not a bit. But then I'm a rather thick-skinned adolescent." She shrugged and William grinned to himself as they walked on.

They went first to Carla's school, where they left her and the wagon with the teacher who met them at the entrance to the building. Then Sarah carried Elizabeth on her arm to the house where the Mrs. Collins lived who cared for the baby during the day. After that William stopped at the elementary school and Sarah walked two blocks farther to Mr. Hager's office, where she began her day's work.

Only, of course, they had all begun the day's work three hours earlier with getting breakfast, doing the dishes, dressing the little children, getting a casserole made for a quick supper when they all came home tired, hanging out a washload of Elizabeth's diapers, seeing that the dogs were fed and watered. These were some of the things that had to be done before work proper began in town.

"Mrs. Cooper says that you're doin' too much, Sarah," Amy reported one evening when Sarah dropped into a chair and sat staring at the pile of fresh vegetables from the garden that had to be washed and made ready for the freezer. "She says that you'll have a breakdown if you don't take things easier—"

Sarah closed her eyes and tilted her head back against her clasped hands. "I'm very fond of Mrs. Cooper," she said raising one eyebrow high into her forehead, "and I'm grateful for her interest, but I wish she'd give us some clear-cut rules for taking things easy and still keeping food on the table." Then when Elizabeth started tuning up for a big scream in the next room, Sarah groaned a little and called out tiredly, "Oh, shut up, baby."

Amy liked Sarah, William believed, but it made Amy feel grown-up when she had a chance to scold. "You're not being a good mother when you yell at her, Sarah. We learned in homemaker's class that infants are very sensitive to harsh words; yelling at them can spoil their lives—"

"Seems to me that Mama told me about a few remarks she made to you after Mary Hand had spoiled you rotten. Do you feel that you carry any scars from that?"

Amy didn't answer. She just lifted Elizabeth from her crib and talked sweet-talk to the baby while she got a bottle of milk from the refrigerator and started to warm it. "Amy loves you, my sweet; Amy's not going to yell at a little wet-bottomed baby that has to cry if she's to get any attention—"

Sarah watched Amy for a minute, a tiny smile at the corners of her mouth; then she looked straight at William and they grinned at one another. Their grins agreed that sometimes Amy was a ham.

There wasn't any doubt, however, about Amy loving the baby. She took over the chore of preparing Elizabeth's formula and the sterilizing of her bottles. Amy would stand over the baby's bed, talking softly to her, getting excited over some gurgle that sounded like a word to no one except Amy. Sarah was afraid that Amy was spoiling Elizabeth, but Amy said no, that the baby needed special love and attention because she was away from her family all day. That made Sarah thoughtful. "I have to be careful," she told William one evening as they picked the first new vegetables of the season together while Amy helped Carla push Elizabeth up and down the front porch in her carriage. "Maybe Amy is right. I don't know enough about babies to be too sure."

William noticed that as the work grew heavier and the days hotter, their tempers were getting shorter and their words sharper—his own included. It was dangerous. Things could fly to pieces awful fast if someone got too mad too suddenly.

One evening when Amy begged off at helping with the dishes because she had to put a hem in the dress she wanted to wear to school the next day, William was furious.

Why couldn't she sew her danged hem before supper? he asked himself as he stood at the sink and plunged his hands into the hot suds. But no. It's a lot better time to do your sewing when there's a pile of dishes to be washed—

Then in the midst of his anger he remembered. What if he and Amy got into one of the big fights they'd had in other years; what if Sarah said, "I can't take it—I'm leaving"; and what if Mr. Hager said, "William will have to go to an orphan place, Amy can go to Mary Hand's in Albany, and we'll send little Carla to that couple in Miami that wanted Elizabeth so much." William closed his eyes for a second and thanked goodness that he'd remembered in time.

The crossness hit Sarah too, sometimes, especially in the evening when they had walked home in the heat and there were still a dozen chores to do before bedtime. She was never cross with Carla, never with William. But several times she lost patience with Elizabeth.

"I recognize a temper tantrum when I meet one, dear little daughter," she told Elizabeth one evening. "You aren't wet and you aren't hungry—you just aren't getting your own way. So go right on yelling for the next two hours and see where it gets you—"

Elizabeth went right on yelling and Sarah wouldn't let Amy pick her up and that made Amy mad. It was very noisy around Mary Hand's house that evening; William took Carla for a walk deep into the quiet woods.

On several occasions Sarah and Amy blew up at one another; they were much better friends than William would ever have expected them to be when Sarah first came, and their little spats ended quickly for the most part. But these quarrels worried William. He was loyal to Sarah and usually saw eye to eye with her. But Amy *was* his sister and he loved her most of the time the way Mama always wanted him to. He didn't want to take sides with either of the big girls; usually he just took off somewhere and waited for the trouble to blow over, but while he waited there was always a dread in his mind.

One of the worst troubles happened on a day when there were no classes in high school and Amy had the chance to stay alone at home all day and do as she pleased. They left the breakfast dishes that morning because Amy said she would wash them later. Sarah asked her if she'd get things started for supper a half-hour or so before the rest of them were due home from town and Amy said yes, of course. No problem.

Amy was in high spirits that morning. She kissed Carla and Elizabeth. She would have kissed William too, but he ducked and told her he wasn't figuring on going to the moon that day. Then Amy linked her arm with Sarah's as they walked out to the gate together. Sarah waved to Amy before she unfolded the purple umbrella, and the express wagon, full of little girls, began creaking down the road.

But that evening when Sarah and William dragged home, dead-tired, and Carla was miserable with the heat and Elizabeth was mad as a wet hen, things weren't so good. The breakfast dishes were still in the sink, the table wasn't set, and there wasn't a sign of supper being started.

Sarah's blue eyes got black as she looked around the kitchen, and she let some parcels fall with a clatter on the worktable. Then, just about that time, Amy came running down the stairs laughing and feeling better than anyone else in the family.

"Oh, you're early—" (they weren't, William thought, but that didn't matter). "I meant to get things done sooner, but I went to sleep this morning and this afternoon I found these. Wait 'til you hear these, Sarah— they're priceless—"

Amy didn't seem to notice the look on Sarah's face, as she went on, "Just listen to this from one of Mary Hand's ancient diaries—'April 7, 1930—It's been a week since I've heard from him. It's nine o'clock now and I have to face something that is very plain: David is never going to call me again—' "

Amy enunciated the last words carefully. "That's underlined," she added. "I guess David got a wrong number or something and our good old Mary Hand had to be an old maid—"

Amy's laughing stopped when she looked up from the book. Sarah was standing straight as a poker, her hands on her hips. William thought she might jump down Amy's throat.

"I was mad just now, Amy, when I saw the dishes in the sink and nothing done toward supper," Sarah said, "but that was nothing, absolutely *nothing*, compared to your reading something never intended for your eyes and to your making fun of Mary Hand. I think what you've done is mean and hateful and cruel—" Sarah stopped with kind of a choking noise while she and Amy looked straight at one another. "And furthermore, if you want to eat supper with us, get down here and do your share—"

Amy started crying, a mad crying that didn't stop her from yelling at Sarah. "I'm not going to eat supper with you—not tonight or ever again. I'm going over to my own dear little house and I'm going to stay there until I can figure out what to do. Maybe I'll starve, but that will be better than staying here and being bossed by somebody that's only three years older than I am—someone that doesn't have any more right to bawl me out than—than Duchess does—"

As Amy started running toward the door, Sarah said "Suit yourself" and turned to do some work at the sink. Amy almost flew across the yard and disappeared into their old house.

William was grateful that Carla was out in the yard walking in the shade with an arm around Nugget's neck. Sarah didn't say anything—just got Elizabeth fed and quieted, and then started picking meat off a pound of chicken wings she had cooked the night before. She washed a damaged box of mushrooms Mr. Cooper had given her and dropped them into a hot skillet where a scoop of margarine had melted; then she asked William to chop up green peppers and onions to be added to the chicken and mushrooms.

"If the 'not likely' ever happens and we have a little extra money, we'll buy sour cream and wine for this chicken dish sometime," she told William as evenly as if cooking something good was the only thing she had on her mind. "That's the right way to do it," she added.

William couldn't find a word to say. He sat down beside Elizabeth's carriage and taking her small hand in his, studied it, as if he expected to find something interesting there.

Sarah went right on talking, determined it seemed to talk about anything except Amy.

"When we were flush Jason would add wine and mushrooms and cream to the chicken. But when we were flat broke—which was most of the time—we just had chicken with onion and peppers. It didn't matter to me. I was always hungry enough to think that anything he cooked was great."

She cooked rice to serve with the chicken, and they had big red tomatoes picked off their own vines. For dessert there was some ice cream for Carla and a bowl of berries for William. Sarah didn't want any dessert that evening.

The food was good and this should have been a fun supper, but of course it wasn't. Carla was plainly puzzled and uneasy; William, although he ate because he was ravenous, found that the chicken and mushrooms had lost much of their flavor. He kept thinking of Amy over in their old house—without supper, without lights or a good bed. All alone too, unless Mama's ghost was there and if it was, it would be sorrowing because there was trouble between Amy and Sarah. It would be afraid that maybe this family was going to pieces.

Sarah hardly touched the food. She pushed her plate back after a while and sat looking at William, leaning her elbows on the table.

When Carla finally went outside to play with Nugget, Sarah spoke in a tired voice. "I've made a mess of something very important, William—"

"You're talking about Amy?"

"Yes. About Amy." She crumpled a piece of bread into little pellets and dropped them on her plate before she went on talking. "Amy and I had some hard days together last fall when we took care of Mama. We came to love one another—like sisters—"

"Then why—?" He stopped short. He knew very well why Sarah had been tough with Amy. She was dead-tired and hot and mad. And here came Amy downstairs, fresh and perky after a lazy day—not caring very much about the dishes in the sink and no supper started, thinking it was funny that some boy had hurt Mary Hand's feelings about a hundred years ago. It made William madder than ever, just thinking about it.

"She's got sense enough to know that what she done was wrong. So why didn't she just tell you she was sorry and get to work helpin' you? She didn't have to run out and talk smart about leavin' forever and starvin' to death—"

"It's called 'saving face,' " Sarah answered thoughtfully. She looked out of the window toward the house next door, seeming to be thinking something over carefully. Then she turned back to him. "I'm mad at Amy, William; in fact I'm just as furious with her now as I was an hour ago. All the same, I know that she can't actually be blamed for walking out. I blasted her. She had to let me know that she was an individual, and so she blasted back—"

"If you was Amy, that's what you'd do, is it?"

"That's what I did do—the year I was sent to the orphanage. I was lonesome and scared those days. I struck back at anyone who dared to bawl me out—to tell me what I could or couldn't do—"

"What had you done to make them bawl you out?" For a minute he forgot Amy's troubles, interested as he was in hearing about the girl Sarah used to be.

"I had run away with two other girls—" She paused and carefully arranged the bread pellets in a ring around the rim of her plate. It seemed like a long time before she went on talking; when she did, the words came very slowly. "When I was brought back, the matron thought she'd make me afraid to do it a second time, but she didn't. Soon as I got a chance, I ran away again—with a much older boy this time—"

She stopped abruptly and William asked the next question without stopping to think whether he should or not. "Is that when Elizabeth started growing inside you?" he asked.

The nod she gave him was just barely a movement of her head. After that, they were silent for a while and when he did speak, William's voice was scared. "Do you think Amy might do something like that, Sarah?"

She didn't answer, just got up and walking over to the stove, started to reheat the chicken she'd left in the kettle. When it was hot, she filled a big plate and found a smaller one for bread and butter and a dish of berries. When everything was ready, she put the two plates on a tray and turned to William. "I know it's not your turn for dishwashing, William, but if you'll do them tonight I won't ask you to go near the sink for the rest of the week." She smiled although her eyes looked troubled. "If there are any problems with Carla or Elizabeth, come over and call me—"

It was a long evening and Carla was irritable. Where was Sarah? Why hadn't Amy eaten supper with them? What was the matter with everybody all of a sudden?

William let her wipe the knives and forks for him and he invented cheerful answers to her questions, pretending that he was content with matters as they stood. He helped her get ready for bed, then he sat beside her and read stories until she grew sleepy. As he leaned over to say good-night, Carla put her arms up to his shoulders. "You didn't fool me, William. I know you got some worries about something—"

"Yes, but they'll all be settled tomorrow, Carla." To himself, he added, "I hope—I very much hope—"

It was almost dark when Sarah and Amy came back to the kitchen. William was seated on the back step brushing a cluster of burrs from Nugget's coat. He pretended to pay little attention to the girls at first, then he grew concerned as Sarah threw herself on the couch beside the screen door and lay there with her eyes closed.

"Today has been a hard one for Sarah—she has a splitting headache," Amy said very quietly, all the loud madness gone from her voice. He remembered Mama saying something about Amy once—"All high winds and rain one hour; all sunshine and little soft breezes the next. That's my Amy—"

"I'll get Elizabeth ready for bed," Amy added. "Let Sarah sleep for a while if she can—"

He walked into the kitchen with his sister. "Is everything all right between you girls?" he asked anxiously.

Amy nodded and in the light he'd left on above the sink, he could see that she'd been crying. "I was a creep, William. It won't happen again—"

"If it does it could blow up our family," he muttered.

"It won't—" She took a cloth from the cabinet drawer and ran cold water over it. "Here, put this on Sarah's forehead. Maybe it will help her—"

He spread the cloth carefully across Sarah's temples. When she didn't speak he went out to the yard and lay on the grass with the dogs beside him. A cool breeze came up and comforted him; after a time he went to sleep.

It was late when he wakened and went back to the porch. Sarah was lying just as he had left her; he hated to disturb her but it seemed right that she should go to her room and rest in a more comfortable bed.

He placed his hand on her shoulder and shook her gently. "You don't want to sleep down here all night, do you, Sarah?" he asked.

She stirred and turned away from him. "Go away," she said shortly, then opening her eyes she seemed to push sleep from them enough to recognize him. "I'm all right, William," she said, taking his hand for a minute, "just bushed. Run along and let me rest a while—" Then she breathed a deep sigh and settled her head deeper into the pillow.

seven

THE NEXT afternoon when school was out William walked over to Carla's school as usual to pick her up and wait for Sarah and Elizabeth to come along. One of the teachers saw him in the hall and came up to speak to him. "Mr. Hager drove by with Sarah and the baby," she told him. "They took Carla with them and Sarah asked that you bring her wagon when you come home."

William hurried home, anxious and wondering as he walked along the dusty road with Carla's express wagon rattling behind him. At home he found Sarah sitting out under the trees with her sketching pad on her lap, but with her hands lying idle upon it. Carla was at her feet playing with Elizabeth on an old quilt.

"What is it, Sarah?" he asked, "has something happened to you?" He noticed that her face still had some of the tiredness of the night before in it, but she looked up at him and smiled.

"I sort of folded up today, William. Mr. Hager thinks I need a day or two of taking it easy, so he brought me and the little girls home this afternoon. It's nothing," she added. "I'll be myself after a good night's sleep."

Amy really came through with being a good kid that evening, William thought. She cooked supper and looked after Elizabeth and wouldn't let Sarah help with the dishes or bathe Carla or fix a casserole for the next night's supper. "William and I are going to take care of you, Sarah," she said, and you'd never have guessed she was the same girl who had bawled and yelled at Sarah the night before. William shook his head as he thought about the changes that had come over Amy in twenty-four hours, and she asked him what was on his mind to cause the headshake.

"Nothin'," he said, and Amy got sassy. "Well, that figures," she said. But her sassiness was good-natured.

William worked for Mr. Cooper that evening, as he often did when work in the garden was lighter and he could find the time. He helped Mr. Cooper unload boxes of fresh vegetables as they were taken from the trucks that drove in from the city. It was tiresome work, especially at the end of the day, but Mr. Cooper paid him well and when the work was done he could run out to the pasture and spend an hour with Blue Streak, the young palomino colt who was just a week younger than Elizabeth.

"You two seem more like brothers than boy and colt," Mr. Cooper said once when he came up to the fence and stood watching as William brushed Blue Streak's coat and fondled the long, sensitive face.

"Someday maybe I can buy him," William said walking over to Mr. Cooper's side. "It's been in my mind a long time that maybe I can save the money I make from this job and from the one with Robert. It just might be that in a year or two I could buy Blue Streak—if you could hold him for me—"

Mr. Cooper put his arm around William's shoulder. "It just might be," he said, "and I promise you, I'll not sell him to anybody else—"

Work was heavy that evening though, and William realized he wouldn't have time to go out to see the colt before dark. All the boxes had to be pried open and great stacks of vegetables placed out for sale the next morning. William had learned to place the freshest ones out front where they made a good showing; then he made the less fresh ones look better by removing bruised leaves and cutting out rotted places from heads of lettuce, by washing smudge stains and sand from grapefruit and oranges. Mr. Cooper complimented him. He said that not many kids could do a job like this as well as William.

At twilight they heard a car coming up the Piney Road. "Looks like there's company from town up at Mary's place," Mr. Cooper remarked, looking out across the truck patches.

"Probably Mr. Hager to see Sarah and talk about the law part of taking care of us," William answered.

He would have liked to go home and be a part of the company evening, but he liked better to earn a little more money while he had the chance. Anyway, Mr. Hager's talk about the records Sarah must keep concerning William and his sisters was often hard to understand and rather boring. Mrs. Hager was pleasant, though she forgot and said the same things over and over every time she saw him—asking him if he knew her grandson Johnny Hager, telling William again and again how much he looked like Mama, wondering just as many times how a sixteen-year-old girl like Sarah was able to paint such a beautiful picture of William. A nice lady but very forgetful, and so he didn't mind too much that he needed to stay on and work while Sarah and Amy talked to the Hagers.

It was quite dark except for starlight when he got home after all the vegetables were washed and set out for next morning's sales. The big girls were in the living room with all the lights on and when they heard him step up on the porch, Amy called excitedly. "Hurry, William. Fantastic newsflash for you—"

She was all smiles and little bounces that would have been a lot of tail wagging if Amy had suddenly been changed to Nugget. He dropped into a chair, too tired to get very excited about anything. Leave the fireworks to Amy, he thought, and looking at her he felt lots older and maybe a bit wiser than his sister.

"Are you goin' to tell me—or do I have to sit up and beg?" he asked, sour as Mr. Cooper when he thought the retail people had cheated on the lettuce shipment.

"We're going to have a car," Amy announced grandly. "A real car, William, not a skate-board, not a cute little toy from the dime store—"

He looked at Sarah, expecting her to wink at him and let him know that Amy was up to some silly prank. "What's the joke?" he asked her quietly.

"It's true, William," Sarah told him. He noticed that her face had lost the droopiness it had shown earlier when he came home from school; tonight it was nearly as bright looking as Amy's. "The Hagers like the portrait I did of you so much that they want me to do one of their grandson. And they'll pay me with a nine-year-old Volkswagen overhauled and polished up and good for another thousand miles or so—"

"They think Sarah's working too hard—and she is," Amy said earnestly, "you and I know that, William, and so today when she almost fainted Mr. Hager got this idea about the portrait and the Volksie for us—"

"Can you drive, Sarah?" William asked, anxious to know that nothing stood in the way of letting this big piece of good fortune come true.

"I know the basics. Jason used to teach me to drive a little when we were out in the country where traffic was light—" She began to count off things things that had to be done, much as she had the night they sipped hot milk together and made plans for the days following Mama's funeral. "First of all, I must pass a driver's test—that won't be hard. After a lesson or two from Robert, I'll be all set. Next, there's insurance. Mr. Hager will pay it for us the first year—after that, we're on our own. Third item, garage. We'll have to rearrange some of the junk Mary Hand has accumulated over the years and stored out there—about a week's work should do it. Fourth item, portrait. What kind of kid is Johnny Hager?"

"Squirrely. He's a good guy, but he can't sit still for five minutes. Every teacher we've had since kindergarten has said that—"

"He'll sit still for me," Sarah said, grim and smiling all at once, "I'm tougher than your teachers—"

They talked for a long time and made plans and were friendly together. When William awoke the next morning he had a feeling that he'd been smiling to himself all night.

Johnny Hager came home with William the next Friday after school and stayed for the weekend while Sarah made sketches of his eyes, his mouth, and every angle of his face as she had done when she painted William's portrait. William warned him that she might do some hard staring—maybe for a long time at nothing more than the shape of his nose.

"It might make you crack up," he told his guest, "but don't let it embarrass you if she gets a little sore. It's a way artists have of keeping their models in line," he added, proud to give Johnny the benefit of his own experience.

Those weeks during which Sarah painted Johnny's portrait held more fun for William than he had known in months. He took Johnny over to see Blue Streak when Sarah dismissed her model for a while, and they raced around the pasture—the colt kicking up his heels and showing off for all the world like a kid who's been lonesome and is suddenly excited at the idea of having company.

"I love this little cuss," Johnny breathed, just above a

whisper, as they stood at the fence stroking Blue Streak's neck, helping him to get over his excitement.

"I know," William answered. They looked at one another. They had been in school together for several years, liking one another well enough—now they were friends.

One night Sarah invited Robert's ten-year-old cousin, Larry, to come out and cook hamburgers with Johnny and William. Amy was nice about getting the food all ready for them to cook, and after supper Sarah helped them pitch an old tent under the pines where the three boys could sleep all night. It was hot in the woods and all kinds of insects were on the rampage—all the same, it was wonderful for three guys to be out there alone, to laugh and yell and scuffle until they were glad to quiet down and sleep. Someone—maybe Mr. Hager—said, "It's what William needs. A sprinkling of his own kind in this family of girls."

The Hagers asked Sarah to do the portrait showing Johnny as if he had just come wading in through the water from a swim, and so they went down to the Gulf where William and Johnny swam and splashed around while Sarah set up her easel on the shore. She did sketch after sketch, sometimes just of the Gulf stretching out to nowhere, sometimes of a soaking-wet Johnny striding up through the shallow waves to the beach, water dripping from every inch of him.

It was a difficult picture for Sarah to paint. "I could do with some help from old Jason on all this water," she told William one day, leaning back to look at the work on her easel, her face showing that she was discouraged. But in a while she was trying again, and for days nothing showed up on her canvas except water—big waves touched with sunlight far out in the Gulf, clear water breaking over pebbles as it came up to the shore, water dripping off a boy's red head and running down to the tip of his nose.

Johnny liked to stand at Sarah's shoulder and watch her paint, but he asked too many questions and finally Sarah turned to William for help. "Take our friend out to the garden and let him help you pick beans, William. He's getting in my hair."

The two boys filled a big basket with beans and carried them in for Amy to wash and put in bags for freezing. Then Johnny couldn't wait to rush out to the yard where Sarah worked at her easel.

"You sure are a slow worker, Sarah," he told her. "Me and William picked a whole basket of beans while you've just painted one measly old ear—"

But Sarah knew how to tease as well as Johnny. She grabbed him when he least expected it, and holding his head firmly under her arm, she dipped a brush in green paint and brandished it above him.

"I'll show you how fast I can paint an ear, young Hager," she said, and a minute later released a green-eared Johnny who raced inside to find a mirror and admire himself.

He was still chortling when all of them gathered around the table to eat the lunch Amy had fixed for them. "I wish I could live out here with you guys," Johnny said, grinning at William. "You have all the fun." He stooped to give Nugget a piece of his sandwich, and while he was busy Sarah turned to Amy.

"That's all we need, isn't it?" she said in a low tone, and Amy made her brows go up in a way that showed how much she agreed.

Sarah took her driver's test and received her license one Friday and on Saturday morning Mr. Hager drove the Volkswagen out to Mary Hand's house, with his wife following in their big car in order to drive her husband back to town. The Volkswagen had been painted a cheerful red and the upholstery had undergone a cleaning that left it looking bright enough to pass for a slightly faded brand-new. It was a beautiful car, William thought, and for the first time in a long while he itched for school on Monday morning.

Finally, after many hours of work on the beach, out in the yard, or upstairs in the room she called her studio, Sarah called Johnny's grandmother and told her that the painting was finished, that she would deliver it the next evening after supper. Mrs. Hager said she was inviting a few neighbors in to see Johnny's portrait, and would Sarah bring all the children and they'd have a small party.

So everybody got cleaned up after supper that evening and ready for a cool drive into town. Amy put on her prettiest dress and she bathed and dressed Elizabeth upstairs while Sarah trimmed William's hair out on the back porch. When that job was done to suit her, she tied a white apron-dress around Carla. "You look very pretty, Carla," she told the slender little girl. William liked her for the way she could make Carla smile and spin around so that her skirts swirled about her.

Then just as everything seemed to be going along fine, Amy had to have a fit when she came downstairs and found that Sarah was wearing an old blouse spattered with a half-dozen different colors of paint and a pair of almost worn-out work shorts.

"Sarah you can't—you simply *can't*—go over to Mrs. Hager's dressed like that," Amy scolded.

Sarah made her eyes open very wide at Amy as if they couldn't understand. "What's the matter with my clothes, Amy? They're *clean*. Anyway, I'm not stepping out into society. I'm just a worker delivering the finished product in payment for our car—"

Amy said that Sarah could be very trying. "And I warn you," she added, "you'll be so ashamed, so humiliated, you'll want to crawl off somewhere and hide. I warn you, Sarah—"

"Do you want to bet?" Sarah asked Amy. Then she laughed and swung herself into the driver's seat of their beautiful little car.

There were a dozen people or more on the lawn and patio at the side of Mr. Hager's house when Sarah drove up in front. William noticed that the ladies were wearing bright summer dresses and that Sarah's old blouse and shorts *did* look very different.

Amy was wrong though, when she said that Sarah would be ashamed and humiliated because of her clothes. Not Sarah, he thought. She walked up the front steps with the same long stride she took when they went for walks in the woods, and she didn't look ashamed or humiliated at all. She smiled her small corners-of-the-mouth smile, and she looked proud of Elizabeth who was plump and rosy in her arms, proud of Carla in her white apron-dress, proud of Amy who looked especially pretty, and proud of William with his fresh haircut and a T-shirt bought in town that morning.

William saw some people looking at Sarah as if they couldn't quite figure her out. He overheard one man say, "Cool little so-and-so, isn't she?" and the lady beside him answered, "A defiant one, I'd say. Attractive though—"

He didn't understand. He only knew they were talking about Sarah and it made him uneasy. He wondered if she saw some of the secret looks that people gave one another after they'd stared hard at her for a while. Well, if she did, it was plain she didn't care two cents for their looks or what they were thinking.

Finally Johnny's grandfather called people to come inside. When everyone was there he held Sarah's painting up against the wall where it was to be hung when it was framed, and there was Johnny, wet hair plastered against his head, a big grin looking as if it might break into a laugh at any minute as he stalked through the water toward the beach. Mr. Hager smiled at Sarah and nodded as he held the painting up for everyone to see.

People looked at Sarah in a different way after they saw Johnny's portrait. They crowded around her, most of them wanting to talk about her father. Some of them told her they had seen Jason West's paintings exhibited in art galleries; one man had read a recent article about her father's work, and he talked on and on about it while other people waited their turn to speak to her.

They wanted to know a lot of things. Wasn't Sarah planning to go to college? Shouldn't she be studying art in some city like New York or Chicago? Wasn't she terribly young to be taking care of a family of children? One lady said surely Jason West's daughter wasn't going to bury herself and her talent out there in the Pine Woods, and Sarah's voice was like something just out of the refrigerator when she answered. William's heart gave a happy jump when he heard her say, "I don't really think I could go to sleep anywhere else, ma'am—"

It was a pleasant enough evening—ice cream and little cakes, an invitation from Johnny's mother to come in and spend the night with Johnny some weekend—everything very nice, but William was wishing to go home long before the party was over.

He felt good finally when they were all settled in their car and on their way home in the moonlight. Amy sat in the back seat with Elizabeth in her arms and Carla leaning against her—all three of them asleep in next to no time. William sat up in front with Sarah, thinking about the fuss people had made over her, feeling anxious and uneasy without quite knowing why.

After a while he said, "Is it stealing when people try to coax somebody away from you?"

Sarah put her hand on his knee and laughed as she answered. "There'll be no stealing in our family, I can promise you. We'll put up a sign saying that all people-stealers will be prosecuted—"

She didn't say anything more for as long as it took to get back to the house. When she stopped the car out in the driveway she leaned down and looked at William very soberly, no laughing now.

"You don't really think, do you, William, that anything people may say will ever make me walk out on my family?"

He shook his head. "I just get scared sometimes," he told her.

eight

AFTER THE Hagers' party lots of people from town began to ask Sarah to paint pictures for them. They had learned not only that Johnny's parents and their guests liked Sarah's work, but also that her father was a painter named Jason West. *That,* William found out, was very important to a lot of people, and *that,* he heard Sarah tell Amy, was a bit of phoniness she didn't care for, but since they needed the money she was willing to overlook it. Not always though. One lady wanted her to sign her picture "Daughter of Jason West," and when Sarah said no, the lady wouldn't accept the finished picture. Sarah laughed a lot as they drove home that afternoon and William was puzzled. They needed the money for that picture to pay for having Mary Hand's ancient refrigerator repaired and buying more art materials for Sarah. He wasn't able to see anything very funny in the lady's behavior.

Sarah had plenty of other orders though. Their telephone rang often that spring, and if the caller wasn't some boy calling Amy, it was someone asking Sarah to do a picture. She could accept only a few orders at a time though; she had plenty of things to do besides painting.

"Why don't you just paint all the time and give up working for Mr. Hager?" Amy asked.

Sarah shook her head. "I'm not all that good yet, Amy. I can almost see Jason crooking an eyebrow at me, if he thought I was getting the genius complex—. All this enthusiasm for my pictures is probably just a flash in the pan for a local gal with a flair for the paintbrushes."

But whether she was good or not, Sarah painted

every spare hour that she could find—portraits mostly, because they were what people wanted. But she grew tired of doing them, and there were days, sometimes weeks, when she painted only pictures that had a special meaning for her—"things that keep bugging me to try them" was the way she put it.

One of these was a watercolor of a window with rain beating against it until the pane looked like pale lead— hurricane rain, William remembered. There was a dim flame of candlelight in the room back of the window, and though a person might not see it at first glance, he could, if he looked carefully, find shadows that made up the faint outlines of a woman's face looking outside.

Amy's eyes got full of tears as she looked at the watercolor. "It's Mama, isn't it?" she asked after a while.

Sarah nodded. "I saw her go to the window so many times that night and stand there looking at the storm outside. The picture's been with me—stamped in my mind, I guess, all of these months—"

Dr. Finley wanted to buy *The Rainy Window* for his study. The three of them, Amy and William and Sarah, stood looking at the watercolor for a long time before taking it out to the car for delivery to Dr. Finley's house. When Sarah spoke, her voice sounded grim. "From now on until I've paid Mary Hand what I owe her, I'll just paint people's children and their pets and their rock gardens—just a lot of pretty pictures—nothing that digs into me the way this one does—"

The months had slipped by since the night of the hurricane, since the morning Sarah told Amy and William that Mama had died while they slept. And the months had added up to years. There had been two gardens to plant each year; oranges to be twisted from their stems for Mr. Cooper's fruit stand; fruit and vegetables to be gathered in, frozen, and preserved for family meals throughout the year. There was work to fill every month of each year—the routine work of fighting weeds and insects and mysterious blights, the weakness of plants that drooped during weeks of drought—plus school problems which erupted now and then, sudden illnesses, sudden angers, an occasional rebellion.

The three years that they had been what William thought of as "a family of kids" had been hard but there were plenty of things worth remembering in those years. Sometimes as he walked in the woods with Duchess and Nugget, William ticked off on his fingers things that made remembering a satisfaction: the palomino colt and a friendship with Johnny Hager that had grown strong partly because of the colt; Elizabeth learning to talk and Carla standing on the stage at school singing to her classmates and a crowd of visitors; winning his letter on the school's basketball team; working with Robert and feeling sometimes that he was Robert's brother; sharing a note with Sarah from a girl named Carole and knowing that Sarah understood his feelings about it—that she was glad. Lots of good things, little and big, crowded out memories of things that were less good—some a lot less than good.

All at once it seemed, Elizabeth and Blue Streak were nearly three years old; Carla was seven, and William had grown to a lanky eleven and a half. The big girls were really grown-up—Amy was sixteen and Sarah nineteen. And all of them had changed, some of them just a little here and there, others a great deal.

Blue Streak and Elizabeth were two who had changed a lot—the colt into a beautiful young horse, graceful and swift enough to live up to his name, and Elizabeth into a talkative little live wire who bounced and wriggled, wasn't above throwing a tantrum now and then, but was for the most part winsome and in love with the world around her.

In spite of the four years' difference in their ages, Carla and Elizabeth were close companions, although Carla sometimes took her role of older sister seriously. "You must mind me, Elizabeth, because Sarah and Amy trust me to take care of you," Carla would say, but Elizabeth resisted minding. She liked to run crazily through the garden and out into the woods, chasing Nugget, singing without ever getting a tune right, sometimes just yelling at the top of her voice.

"My little sister is wild," Carla liked to tell visitors. "We got her in a hurricane—that's why."

But Amy was the one who had changed the most. She was getting prettier each year, at least Mrs. Cooper thought so—and Sarah and Johnny Hager's mother. William remembered how he used to get mad at Mary Hand for playing the same old record about Amy's looks over and over again, but now he found himself pleased, sometimes even proud, to hear people talk about how pretty his sister was, how popular she was in high school. He liked Amy—she had her faults, but on the whole, he liked old Amy quite a lot.

One morning when they had time to treat themselves to a late breakfast, Sarah sat at the table looking at Amy with that steady look she had given both William and Johnny before she began painting them.

"I'd like to do your portrait, Amy," she said.

Amy was pleased at first. "You would?" she squealed, then suddenly remembered something she didn't like. "Oh, Sarah, you *would* have to think of painting me right now with this short haircut." She shook her head. "I'm sorry. you can't do it right away. Not 'til my hair gets long again—"

Some friends of hers had finagled her into getting a short, short haircut the week before, and she'd been mad about it ever since. She fussed as if the length of her hair really amounted to something, though, in William's opinion, it wasn't worth wasting one's breath about.

Sarah hadn't paid much attention to Amy's beefing either, but this morning she said, "Short hair shows off your oval face, Amy—actually it's flattering. I like it."

"Thank you. Sorry that I don't share your opinion," Amy answered pertly.

Sarah pushed her chair back suddenly and went upstairs to her room. "Now I suppose she's mad because I dared to defend my own taste," Amy said, looking after her.

"Maybe she's just fed up with talk about your silly hair," William remarked. "It gets tiresome, if you ask me."

Amy shrugged and glared at him in silence. Neither of them spoke further until Sarah came downstairs carrying a small leather box which she handed to Amy.

"Maybe these will help you like your haircut better. If they do, you can have them."

Amy opened the box and lifted out a pair of gold hoops, the kind girls fasten to their ears. She gave a little gasp as she held them up. "Do you actually mean you'll *give* them to me—you'll hand them over just like that?"

Sarah nodded. "Without strings," she said curtly.

"But Sarah, think it over—they're beautiful. Don't you want them yourself?"

"No, I don't want them," Sarah said very quietly.

"Did someone give them to you?" William could see that Amy was going to ask too many questions. He wished to heaven she would shut up, though he was pretty sure she wouldn't. Amy was bright in school subjects, but not in seeing when she was rubbing people the wrong way.

"Yes," Sarah answered. Her voice was getting icy, but Amy barged right on.

"A boy?" Amy guessed.

"That's right, Amy."

"The boy that's Elizabeth's father—is that the one, Sarah?"

Sarah walked out on the porch where Carla and Elizabeth were playing. "Would you girls like to take a walk with Sarah this morning?" she asked, taking each of them by the hand. When they reached the steps, she looked back. "If you like the earrings, Amy, you can have them. I don't care to talk any more about them." She closed the screen door firmly as she left the porch.

Amy watched them as they disappeared into the woods. "Well!" she said finally, "how high-hat can you get at a minute's notice?"

She leaned her elbows on the table and supported her face in her hands. After a while she looked up at him. "You like her, don't you, William?"

"Yes," William answered. He supposed now Amy would make something of it and they'd have a big fight.

Amy, however, was unusually quiet. "You don't get sore at anything she says or does, do you?"

He shook his head. "I can't remember that I ever have," he said.

Amy nodded slowly. "Neither did Mama." She stared out at the empty house across the yard for a minute. "I know I ought to like Sarah," she said after a while, "and usually I do. I know she does a lot for us. Dear Robert makes a point of telling me that every time he knows I'm mad at her. He and Sarah both burn me up sometimes— acting so superior when they're only a few years older than I am—"

"Could be you're a little uptight about them," William muttered. But she evidently didn't hear him, which was just as well. He just sat there quietly drumming his fingers on the table the way Robert did when he had a problem. Finally he said, "Well, are you going to let her paint your picture or not?"

Amy didn't answer, just got up with a sassy little twist of her body and went out to look into the small mirror Mary Hand had always kept hanging on the porch to show a person just coming in from work whether he looked decent enough to sit down at the table or not. She turned her head from one side to the other, looking carefully at herself from every angle. After a while she turned toward him and smiled.

"My face *is* oval, isn't it, William?"

"Could be." He sighed and decided to do some weeding out in the garden. Sometimes it was a pleasure to yank weeds out of the soil and feel peace and quiet all around him.

Amy was not long in deciding to have her portrait painted. "After all, Sarah, you are an artist. You must know better than I do whether my hair is right for a portrait," she said sweetly when Sarah returned to the house. "I think I'd like for you to paint me—that is, of course, if you really want to—"

"Otherwise I wouldn't have mentioned it," Sarah said, and began setting up her easel and getting her sketch pads out.

Amy was a good model, considerably better, William realized, than either he or Johnny had been. Sarah allowed him to watch as she sketched Amy from many angles, but the sketching became monotonous as she studied her work and tried over and over again. William grew impatient after a time, but when the painting began he watched, fascinated, as Amy's toast-brown face slowly came to life, her eyes and dimples and curving mouth all set for laughter as she peeped out through a tangle of leaves and hibiscus flowers that hid the rest of her body.

It was a bright painting, glowing with the colors that Sarah thought were right for Amy—cerise and gold, umber and ochre and burnt sienna—all of which she named for William as each was brought into use; then he watched in amazement as every separate color was lost in a blending and shading of all of them.

Everybody helped during the time Sarah needed for the painting. Spring gardening was heavy and work had to go on as usual, although some of the things they'd always called "must-chores" were simply overlooked for a while. The dogs' coats were not brushed free of burrs and fleas each night, the rooms upstairs didn't get the weekly airing Mama had taught William and Amy to give them. Once in a while when everyone was dead-tired, the supper dishes went unwashed until morning.

"We'll reform as soon as we have Amy done in oil," Sarah said, and painted eagerly during every hour she could take from the garden, the kitchen, and the care of Elizabeth and Carla.

"Will you sell Amy when she's finished, Sarah?" Elizabeth asked one day. She was accustomed to seeing pictures wrapped up for delivery, to having Sarah tell her "This is for money to buy shoes for you, a raincoat for Carla, and ice cream for both of you when you've been good enough for a treat—"

This time, however, Sarah laughed and shook her head. "No, we're going to hang Amy above the fireplace and keep her with us," she said. Amy smiled at that and put her arm around Sarah's shoulders for a second before walking over to take her place in the model's chair.

Amy was proud of her picture—maybe too proud— William thought, seeing her stand before the painting for long minutes, a dreamy look in her eyes as if nothing on earth mattered except that girl Sarah had painted among the flowers. He remembered a time when Mama had scolded Amy for stopping too often in front of the mirror, smiling and turning her head from side to side after she'd heard someone talking about how pretty she was. He wondered about Amy, but then he decided to relax. Amy was older now. She had too much good sense to turn into a silly peacock.

A lot of people came in to see the portrait—all the Hagers and Robert's parents, who had known Amy all her life; the Coopers came over, of course; and the Finleys. Even a few strangers stopped by because they'd heard of Sarah's work. And dozens of Amy's classmates biked out from town, admiring the portrait first, then exploring the gardens, the empty house next door, and the woods. A few of them went down to the pasture with William where he was proud to introduce them to Blue Streak—to boast a little about owning the colt some day if things went well.

As they walked back from the pasture, a girl named Carrie Wright who had hardly given Blue Streak a second glance, stopped to look around her as if what she saw was something special. She had long blonde hair that hung down to her waist, and that was pretty; her mouth, though, was painted a strange kind of purple, and that, William thought, was anything but pretty. She linked arms with Amy and spoke as if a thought had suddenly exploded.

"Look, Saunders, this place is perfect for a bash. Why don't you have some of us out this weekend?" She smiled at Amy then, a sly-looking purple smile that William didn't like. "Maybe though, the artist wouldn't go for that—what do you think?"

At that Amy—who had lately seemed fond of Sarah and very nice to her—got pert, telling Carrie Wright that she did whatever she pleased about inviting her friends out here whether "the artist" liked it or not. Her expression was high and mighty as she spoke, but when she saw William looking hard at her, the expression toned down a little. "I'll say this for Sarah, though—she's really quite nice most of the time. I think she'd be glad to have the kids out some evening—" Amy didn't look either at Carrie Wright or William as she spoke.

Amy didn't mention a party until Saturday morning. "A few of the kids want to come out tonight, Sarah, not many—six or eight. You don't mind, do you?"

Sarah shook her head. "They're *your* guests, Amy. I'll be glad to help you though, if I can. Shall I bring home Cokes when I drive William to work?"

Amy got bubbly with delight. "Oh, Sarah, you *are* nice—and I'm so grateful. I'll do all the dishwashing next week without a beef. I promise you faithfully, I will."

Sarah seemed happy as they drove into town. "Why don't you ask Robert if he'll come out and help you and me host Amy's friends tonight?" she said as she stopped the car in front of the place where William and Robert were going to work that day.

But Robert had other plans for that night. He said to tell Sarah he was sorry; but somehow, William thought, he didn't look sorry—thoughtful, but not sorry.

By eight that evening the motorcycles and cars began roaring up the dusty road and turning in at Mary Hand's driveway. And there weren't just six or eight kids—something more like sixteen or eighteen.

There hadn't been so much noise around Mary's house since the night of the hurricane; only this time it was loud talking and laughing which confused Elizabeth and Carla and left William feeling lonely, barely tolerated by the sixteen-year-olds swarming over the place.

Sarah looked as thoughtful as Robert had, William

noticed, and not too happy, although she seemed to be trying to keep cool and be polite. But blackness covered the blue part of her eyes when a kid named Ronnie Pike asked her loudly if numbers hadn't helped her in painting Amy's picture. "Come on now, kiddo, come clean," he said grinning. Sarah didn't like being called "kiddo," and she didn't like the insult which suggested she knew nothing about painting. She turned her back on Ronnie Pike and walked out of the room as if she needed to get away in a hurry.

She was friendly though with lots of other kids. When a girl spilled Coke in the living room, Sarah got a basin of cold water and helped her rinse the stain out of Mary Hand's good carpet while she laughed and made jokes so the girl wasn't too embarrassed. Later when a boy almost as tall as Robert asked her to dance with him, Sarah said yes, of course, and if you weren't pretty sure that she was worried about all the noise and the night getting later and later, you might have thought she was having a great time.

William had been up at six that morning and had helped Robert through a long day with the lawn work in town. He was bushed and as the hours went on he wondered drearily how you get people headed for home when you're sick and tired of them. He felt lonely as if the two familiar houses and the gardens and woods had been overtaken by a band of strangers who ignored him and behaved as they pleased, acting as if they had every right. As he walked through the yards and gardens he saw two couples drinking from a bottle on the porch of his old home; down in the woods path, Carrie Wright and some boy stood kissing one another.

William turned away and walked back to the house. He sat down in a corner of the living room feeling angrier than he had ever felt in his life and, at the same time, completely helpless to do anything about his anger. It was while he was sitting there that he suddenly saw Carla standing at the foot of the stairs.

She had evidently grown frightened by the noise and had come downstairs to find one of the three older ones in her family. Before William could reach her side she ran forward, stumbling over a camera that Ronnie Pike had placed on the floor beside his chair. As Carla fell to the floor, Ronnie's prized possession went crashing with a sharp bang into the opposite wall.

William picked his sister up and faced Ronnie who was yelling at her as if she were a boy his own age. The thought ran through William's mind that Carla had never been yelled at in all her life.

"If that clumsy brat has ruined my camera you're goin' to pay for it, Saunders—you or the big-shot artist, one of you—"

"She didn't see your lousy camera—Carla is blind—" William choked over the word he and Amy and Mama had always hated to say.

"I don't care if she's deaf and dumb—or just a stupid moron," Ronnie screamed. "If that camera is ruined, you're goin' to pay for it—"

The boy who had danced with Sarah and a couple of others took over at that minute. "You're drunk, Pike, and you're obnoxious," one of them told Ronnie. They took him by the shoulders and dragged him out into the yard where everybody quieted down suddenly except Ronnie, who swore and screamed, and the two dogs, who yelped in excitement. After a few minutes the cars and motorcycles of Amy's friends got into action; but before they left several kids came back to the living room to apologize to Amy and Sarah. Carrie Wright didn't bother to say so much as good-bye before she left, William noticed.

When the place was finally quiet again, William went upstairs to his room. He saw that Amy was crying out on the porch; and he had a glimpse of Sarah standing at the door of the room where she had carried Carla back to bed, her hands pressed on either side of her face.

Up in his room William sat in the darkness for a long time, trembling with anger and with something else he couldn't quite explain at first. Finally he realized that it was a dread of things that might be happening later, of other parties like this, of the Carrie Wrights and Ronnie Pikes that could tear the family in Mary Hand's house all to pieces.

The next morning he was wide awake at dawn and in spite of his tiredness, he wanted to get up, to go out to see the colt, maybe to do some thinking beside the old boulder in the woods. As he walked through the yard he picked up two beer cans and an empty whiskey bottle. He accepted the litter indifferently, too tired to get mad all over again.

As he walked back of the empty house toward the trash cans, he saw Mr. Cooper coming slowly across the truck path looking pretty tired himself. When he came up he looked at William steadily.

"That was a loud party last night, William," he said. No smile that morning such as he usually had for any of his neighbors next door.

William breathed deeply. "Yes, I know how bad it sounded, Mr. Cooper."

"Not only sounded bad, was bad, huh? Kids drinkin', wasn't they?"

"Some of them—not all—"

"Amy's sidekicks?"

"Yes. A big bunch of them—"

"Sounded like a fight toward the last?"

William told him about the Ronnie Pike incident,

how some of the boys dragged Ronnie outside when he screamed at Carla.

Mr. Cooper was silent for a while. Then he said, "Sarah didn't try to put a stop to all this?"

"Sarah didn't know about the drinking—and she wasn't in the room when Ronnie got mean. Don't blame Sarah, Mr. Cooper. That bunch was out of hand. They wouldn't have paid any attention to her—"

Mr. Cooper looked at the ground and shook his head slowly. "That's the thing that worries me, William. If Sarah's too young to take charge of things like this, I'm afraid—" He stopped speaking and William's heart raced.

"What are you afraid of, Mr. Cooper?" he managed to ask.

"I'm afraid you children better not live out here alone. We've all knowed it was risky business, but your mother was so set on it—she had such hope that Sarah could keep all of you together at least 'til Amy was through high school. Well, I don't know—" He put his hand on William's shoulder. "We'll wait and see. I'll have a talk with Hager later on. Maybe he ought to talk with Amy and Sarah—both of them—"

William stood unmoving as he watched their neighbor out of sight. Then he threw the litter he'd picked up into a trash can and went inside the little house, where he sat in the one chair left in the living room—finding no comfort in being there but preferring the familiar look of the living room to anything outside.

After a long time he heard Carla and Elizabeth laughing over their breakfast and he was glad that Carla had forgotten her fear—that maybe she remembered it all as a bad dream. A little later he saw Sarah help the two little girls into the Volkswagen and then drive out into the narrow road that wound through the woods on her way, he was sure, to the lake that lay on the other side. She often did that. It was restful, she told him once, to let the children play in the sand while she sat alone thinking her own thoughts.

Amy came to the kitchen door shortly after Sarah left and called him several times to come to breakfast, but he didn't answer her. He wasn't sure that he ever wanted to talk to Amy again, maybe sometime but the memory of the night before would have to grow a lot dimmer in his mind.

Finally Amy crossed the yard and came into the room where he was sitting. "Didn't you hear me calling you?" she asked as she came inside.

"I'm not deaf," he answered.

"But you *are* pretty much the smart aleck for a kid only just eleven years old," she said.

"Don't make me madder than I am already, Amy. Maybe you're so gung-ho about your pals that you don't mind seeing Carla scared by a drunk punk the way she was last night—"

"Do you think *I* liked it, William? I'd never have invited Ronnie Pike out here—never. Or a lot of the other kids either. Carrie took it on herself to advertise the party to that mob—I only asked six or seven kids I specially liked—"

"Then why don't you tell Carrie Wright to go fall in the Gulf the next time she tries to cook up something with you?"

Amy looked distressed. "She's been nice to me—lots of times—" she said weakly.

William didn't answer. A weakness was spreading through him, something full of fear. When he started to speak it was hard for the words to get past that weakness.

"Something like last night is going to break us up,

Amy," he said at last. "They won't let us live here with Sarah. Mr. Cooper almost said that this morning—" He rubbed tears out of his eyes before he went on talking. "The night of the hurricane we wondered what was going to become of us, remember that? And now we have to begin wondering again—"

Amy cried then. Of course, she always cried and people always forgave her. Then she'd be good for a while, and then she'd do something that shook everybody as much as ever. This time she was saying, "I'll go see Mr. Hager, William. I'll tell him that there'll never be a party like last night again. I'll apologize to Mr. and Mrs. Cooper for the noise and some of the kids drinking. I'll make everything right, William. You can trust me."

nine

AMY AND SARAH went into town the next day and talked for a long time with Mr. Hager about the party and about the five of them going on being a family together. Amy told William about it that evening when they walked down through the woods together at dusk.

"Sarah stood up for me, William. She wasn't mad at me the way you were—" Amy gave him a reproachful look as she let that statement sink in. "Actually she was like a sister, like a dear, understanding friend. I'll never forget the way she explained to Mr. Hager that the trouble was not my fault—"

"Why don't you cut out the flowery stuff and just tell me what happened?" William interrupted, a touch of vinegar in his voice.

"I thought you'd be pleased that Sarah and I are friends—"

"I am. So what did Mr. Hager say about all of us living out here?"

"Well, he wants us to go on the way we are. He said that was what Mama wanted and so does he. Then he said no more parties like the one the other night on account of you and the little girls and on account of Sarah's and my good names. I told him that I'd never in a hundred years have let Ronnie and some of the others come out here if I'd known how gross they could be and he said, 'I believe you, Amy.'" She looked at William proudly as she repeated Mr. Hager's words. "Some people have confidence in me, dear brother," she added.

William's face relaxed into a near-smile. "So?" he said when she paused. "Then it's all settled?"

"Well, we made a few plans. Mr. Hager says, of course, a girl my age should have some social life. He says Sarah needs some too, but she just shrugged her shoulders. Then he said when I go out that I should tell Sarah where I'm going and tell her who I'm going with and when I plan to be home. And if I see I'm going to be a little late I should call Sarah and tell her because Mr. Hager says that she's too young to get wrinkles in her face over worrying about me, and that's perfectly true, William. From now on I'm going to think of Sarah and not of myself all the time—" Amy stopped, out of breath, looking very much the good girl. Ready to sprout wings, William thought.

He talked to Robert about Amy one afternoon as they took a long drive into the country to see what trees and shrubs were needed for a lawn surrounding a newly built house. "She's nicer to Sarah than she's ever been before and lately she's been behaving herself," William reported cheerfully.

Robert nodded. "I hope it lasts," he said. He looked, William noticed, as if he had his doubts.

"You don't like Amy much anymore, do you, Robert?" he asked anxiously.

Robert's eyes were on the road ahead. "Oh, yes, I like Amy," he said quietly.

"Mr. Hager told Sarah that we have to have confidence in Amy," William said, reproach in his voice.

"That advice must have made Sarah's day for her."

After a while William ventured to say something which he feared was out of line, but which was something he wanted to get off his mind.

"I wish she was going out with you, Robert," he blurted. Immediately he wished he hadn't said it.

Robert laughed a short, angry laugh that proved William's words were, indeed, out of line. "No, that's out.

Amy hasn't a very high regard for a guy who's been taking night classes for four years and driving a truck instead of a flashy car. She's sure that I'm some kind of a jerk, and I'm just as sure that she's a shallow, immature little girl right now." After a while he added, "She needs you dad and mother—she'd listen to them. But not me. Amy has trouble remembering my name these days—"

"She remembers that you haven't come out to see her picture. I heard her say something about it to Sarah—"

Robert nodded. "I've been afraid I'd have to stand in line—"

William quietly studied Robert's face for the next few minutes. "This is the first time I've ever seen you look mad, Robert."

Robert smiled at that, the familiar friendly look coming back into his eyes. After a minute he asked about Carla and Elizabeth. "I'll run out and see them sometime this week," he said. "I found two little rocking chairs in unfinished wood the other day. As soon as I've sanded them I'll put on some varnish and bring them out to the young ladies."

Robert was a welcome visitor a few nights later when he brought out the chairs for the little girls and sat on the grass with William and Sarah, talking easily and never seeming to notice that Amy was not there. "She's wrestling with Spanish grammar tonight," Sarah apologized, "she'll probably be down later—"

But Amy didn't show up and after an hour or so, Robert got up and extended his hand to Sarah to help her to her feet. "I must have a look at the new painting now," he said. "I think everybody in town has seen it except me."

Inside the living room Robert walked over to the fireplace and looked up at the picture. From the top of the stairs Amy called hello and Robert asked, "How's the

Spanish subjunctive coming along?" but she had disappeared in a flash and didn't answer.

Robert looked at the portrait for a long time without speaking, then finally turned to Sarah, smiling but puzzled. "I never get over being amazed, Sarah, that a girl I know—somebody who hoes potatoes and tears around town in an old Volkswagen—has this talent cooped up somewhere inside her."

William heard the floor squeak once in the hall upstairs. He remembered how he and Amy used to stand at one side of the landing and eavesdrop when Mary Hand was making plans for Christmas with Mama—plans the two eavesdroppers weren't supposed to hear. He was fairly sure now that Amy was up there listening, waiting to hear what Robert had to say about the painting.

Robert and Sarah talked for quite a long time about it. He wanted to know any number of things about painting—how the portrait was started, how it developed, how the colors were deepened and made rich. He would listen to Sarah for a while, then turn back to look at the picture again. He thought that someday when he could afford it he'd like to have Sarah do a painting for him—something with the same bright colors that glowed in this last picture.

There wasn't a word, however, about the pretty girl with the mischievous smile who looked out from the tangle of leaves and bright flowers in the portrait.

He guesses that she's waiting for some of the compliments she's been getting lately, William thought. He didn't care too much that Robert was giving Amy a taste of the indifference she knew how to dish out so well. Still, Robert was a part of their old life with Mama. William wondered if Amy might be feeling lonesome as she stood alone upstairs, and waited to hear Robert say that she looked pretty in the picture.

Amy was quiet and aloof the next morning. When Elizabeth pulled her out on the porch to see the new rocking chairs, she said yes, dear, very nice—and that was all. Then she told Sarah in an icy voice that she didn't care for breakfast and went up to her room to get ready for school. Sarah and William did all the morning chores together that day.

"Why don't we call her to come down and do her share?" William asked, nettled by the extra work and the injustice of it.

"Let's wait a few hours for the weather to change," Sarah answered, "things may be rosy by tonight."

William, now in junior high school, had classes next to Amy and so they got out of the car together when Sarah stopped in front of the high school. "What's buggin' you, Amy?" Willian asked as soon as they were alone. "You didn't come down to be friendly with Robert last night, and now this morning—"

"I didn't come down to be friendly with Robert last night because it was plain that he and Sarah had so much in common. I didn't want to interrupt his sudden interest in art—" She turned away abruptly and hurried off to link arms with Carrie Wright without another look at her brother.

It turned out, however, that Sarah had made an accurate weather prediction. By that evening, everything was rosy; Amy was excited and eager, nice to everybody, doing her share of the work enthusiastically. The reason for the change was, as William suspected, a special date and a special party coming up for the weekend.

"His name is Brandon Hillyard," Amy told Sarah. "He's a freshman over at the junior college—terribly good-looking and much more mature and sophisticated than that crowd out here the night of the disaster party—" She hesitated and laughed self-consciously. "I know this sounds conceited, Sarah, but he's told a lot of kids I know that I'm the prettiest girl in either high school or junior college."

"Sounds as if he has good taste—and that he's been doing a lot of looking around." Sarah smiled and handed Amy a pail. "Well, let's get the peas picked tonight before they're too hard. Mr. Cooper told me yesterday that we'd better get them gathered or they'd lose their sweetness—"

They were talking about a dress for Amy that night when William got back from the pasture where he'd gone to ride for a while on Blue Streak. Sarah had found a white dress of her own in the closet. It had grown yellow with hanging unused so long, but she thought a night's soaking in bleach water would bring back the whiteness. "Then we can shorten it," she told Amy, "and I'll cut out a bunch of petals and leaves from some bright scraps in Mama's sewing basket. I'll show you how to sew them on to look like a big corsage on your shoulder—"

Robert drove William home after work on the evening before Amy's party. "I came to hang the swing I promised the kids last week," he told Sarah, rolling a big tire out of his truck and uncoiling a length of rope.

She was pleased and while William and Robert hung the swing from a low branch of one of the shade trees, Sarah brought sandwiches and a pitcher of iced tea out so they could all sit in the shade and eat together.

Robert had just come up on the porch to carry a tray down for Sarah when Amy walked out, looking beautiful as the girls on magazine covers, her white skirt swirling around her knees, short hair lying close to her head showing off a face that was, indeed, oval.

Robert looked at her without smiling as she stepped out on the porch, then he said "Hi, Amy" very quietly and she said "Hi" suddenly looking mad, William noticed—like maybe she'd expected Robert to say she looked like a million.

Amy turned her back without another word to Robert and spoke to Sarah. "I'll be a little late tonight, Sarah, but I'll call you around midnight and let you know when I'll be home—" She shrugged her shoulders slightly as she turned away from Sarah. "Do run along now for your picnic. You make a charming family scene, all of you seated on the greensward—" she added in a certain kind of voice. Malicious, William believed, was the name for this particular kind of voice.

They heard Amy's date drive up in front and Amy's voice calling out a greeting as she ran down the steps.

"They're leaving early," Robert said.

"Yes, Amy says the boy wants her to meet his parents. Then two or three couples are going for a swim before the party begins," Sarah explained.

"Who *is* this kid?" Robert asked as the car roared away from Mary Hand's gate as if it was behind time for something important.

"His name is Brandon Hillyard, freshman at the junior college. The party is at his home—a big place on the outskirts of town, I understand—"

"Interesting," Robert said, grim as he'd been a few weeks before when he and William had talked about Amy. "*Very* interesting because the senior Hillyards are up in Maine for the summer months. I talked to Ed Hillyard about a week ago and he told me they were leaving the next day."

Sarah didn't say anything for quite a long time. Then she asked, "Do you know young Hillyard?"

"By reputation. A spoiled brat with a taste for—" Robert paused, then added, "a number of things that Amy shouldn't be tasting."

Sarah kept staring at Robert. There was a helpless look in her face, helpless and scared. "I wish I had known, Robert."

"You should let Hager or me know when she takes on a new acquaintance—"

Sarah sighed as she looked up at him. "Robert, I can't destroy Amy's trust in me by going behind her back. I can't report every move she makes or get a character check on all her friends. Mr. Hager told me that we have to have confidence in her—"

"I know. Hager thinks she's still Libby's sweet little girl. Well, she's a big girl now, and not always so sweet—" He frowned and his voice was harsher than William had ever heard it.

"She didn't tell you that Hillyard's parents are out of town?"

"I don't suppose she knew—"

"You trust her more than I do, Sarah."

Sarah jumped to her feet and faced Robert angrily. "Look, Robert, you know as well as I do that I have no authority over Amy. She knows it too, believe me. I see it in her eyes every time we disagree on any little thing. Amy knows that I'm not in a position to take the place of her mother or her guardian. I'm not even an older friend with an unblemished record—"

Robert got up and put his hands on Sarah's shoulders. "You're the best friend Amy's ever had—I hope she'll wake up to that before it's too late—" He stood there, just looking at Sarah. "I realize that I'm not helping you by sounding off. It's just—just that I've heard things about Hillyard and his pals that I don't like. I'm scared, Sarah—"

She nodded. "So am I—" She hesitated then and glanced at William. "But only a little bit," she added. "It could be that we're getting on edge over nothing. Come on. Let's help the girls get used to their new swing—"

She called the children and for the next half-hour the air was full of their excited cries as they tried out the swing, growing bolder with each push they were given.

"Make me go higher, Robert—higher still—" Elizabeth yelled, but he wouldn't. "Let's not be too brave too soon," he said. He looked tired as he lifted her out of the swing to give Carla one more turn.

"What time did she say she'd call?" he asked Sarah when Carla chose to swing slowly by herself.

"Around midnight. She's been faithful about calling since Mr. Hager talked to her about it—"

"I'm going to be studying until late tonight. Maybe I'll drive out here when I'm through. If she gets home earlier, turn the porch light off so I'll know everything's all right—"

Sarah looked up at him and shook her head slightly. "Robert, is it really as serious as all that?" she asked.

"Yes," he said. "To me it is—"

They watched his truck move down the dusty road and then walked silently back into the house. "I'll get the girls ready for bed—I suppose they'll hold me to reading a story if they remember this is Saturday night—" Sarah stopped at the foot of the stairs. "I wish we had called Johnny or some of your friends and asked them to come out for the night. You boys could have had another 'sleep out' in the woods."

"No, I'm glad I don't have company tonight," William answered. "Somehow I just don't feel like havin' people around."

"I may be reading most of the evening. I have a book that looks interesting—"

He nodded. "That's all right. You go ahead and read. I don't want to go upstairs though. I'll stay down here with you as long as you're up if you don't mind—"

"No, I don't mind," she said, "glad to have someone around."

He roamed around the place for a while, lonesome and pretty blue, until he thought of the palomino and what a gallop would be like through the woods and over to the hard-packed bridle path along the Gulf shore. Mr. Cooper never refused to let him ride Blue Streak. "He'll by yours, William, one of these days; the two of you might as well have some fun together while you're both young."

The Gulf was gentle that evening—like someone old and kind who understood how you felt and liked you. The slow wind that drifted in over the water was gentle too, cool and refreshing. The palomino walked quietly along the shore after its gallop through the woods, seeming to feel the same serenity that had come to William now that he was alone and removed from the troubles of Robert and Sarah and Amy.

When he returned to the house William found Sarah reading in the living room. He picked up a hassock and carried it close to her chair. "Are you worried, Sarah?" he asked.

"Not a lot," she answered. "Robert had me upset for a while, but I think Robert is going overboard a little. He would be mad and worried, no matter what boy Amy went out with. He's like some fathers—there isn't any guy good enough for the girl he loves—"

William looked at her in surprise. "Don't think for a minute that Robert loves Amy, Sarah. Maybe he did when she was little, but not anymore. He practically told me that he didn't—"

Sarah laughed. "Don't let Robert kid you, William. He'd like to wring her neck, I expect, but he's very fond of Amy—"

William sighed. "I don't get it," he said quietly, then

decided to drop the subject altogether. "Don't you want to read?" he asked after a while.

She snapped the light off and laid the book on a table beside her. "Not if you'd rather talk," she said.

For a while he wondered what to talk about, but finally he said, "You and Amy don't care about the same things, do you?"

"You're thinking about parties and dates?" she asked.

"I guess so."

"I'm older than Amy, you know—"

"But you're not really old—Robert thinks you ought to go out with people your own age and have a good time. Don't you ever *want* to do that?"

She answered right away as if she didn't need to stop and think things over. "No, I really don't, William. Mrs. Hager would agree with Robert—she thinks I'm too young to be living as I am. What they don't understand is how safe I feel down here. I'm a little afraid of the outside world and people, I guess—"

"I didn't think you were afraid of anything."

"I am though. Ever since Jason died I've been afraid until—until Mary Hand let me come down here to hide—and you and Mama let me know you liked me—" She paused for a while and then added, "Having you kids with me—having a chance to paint—is enough for me. It's come to be a kind of—I don't know how to say it—kind of a security blanket, I guess."

He thought about her words as they sat in the darkness together. "The best thing that ever happened to me was you coming down here," he said softly. "You're the best thing in my life since Mama died."

Sarah didn't answer for a minute; then she said, "Why don't you stretch out on the couch for a while and get some sleep? I'll let you know when Amy calls."

He went to sleep immediately. Saturdays were long workdays with Robert; William looked forward to them, but he was always tired by bedtime on Saturday night.

The lights were still on in the living room when he was awakened by Robert coming up to the front door. He heard Robert say, "She's not home yet?"

"Not yet." Sarah's voice sounded tight.

"No call?"

"No."

"It's after two o'clock."

"I know it."

"I have half a mind to drive out there and make her let me bring her home—"

"We're both tired, Robert. After all, Amy's staying out until after two o'clock isn't exactly unheard-of behavior. Those kids probably don't realize it's after midnight—"

"And, of course, she doesn't realize that she hasn't called you as she promised. After all, it's none of our business. I wish—" Robert added angrily, "I wish I didn't give a damn what she does, what little rotter she's out with, or when she gets in—"

Sarah put her hand on his shoulder. "Try to get some rest, Robert. I'll call you the minute she comes home."

Robert left shortly after that, and Sarah went back to her book. William lay watching her for a while; he noticed that she turned the pages slowly and seemed to be interested in what she read. After a while he went back to sleep.

Late, late in the night he heard their telephone ring. He heard Sarah say, "I called the Hillyard home a few minutes ago and asked for Amy. Somebody made a lewd remark and banged the receiver in my ear—" She listened for a while and then spoke again. "Yes, I think that at four o'clock in the morning we have a right to expect a sixteen-year-old girl to be getting home—'' Then she took a deep breath and said ''Thank you, Robert'' before she hung up.

William got up from the couch, the words ''four o'clock in the morning'' filling him with a cold fear for Amy. He'd heard a lot about drugs that drove kids crazy; he knew about a thing called rape that happened to girls sometimes. Almost every week the papers had stories about some girl being raped and murdered, buried in a lonely place where she wasn't found for weeks.

Sarah was standing at the window with her back to him. He went over to her side and clutched her wrist. ''Sarah, do you think something has happened to Amy?'' he asked.

She took his hand. ''We'll try not to borrow too much trouble, William. I think maybe Amy is just telling Mr. Hager and Robert and me that she's going to do as she pleases—'' Sarah smiled wearily. ''She's probably quite all right—feeling much better than we are—''

''Is Robert going to make her come home?''

''He's going to try. There may be trouble though, with some of Amy's friends—they were noisy when I called—''

''What's a 'lewd remark,' Sarah?'' he asked after a while.

''A dirty one.''

''It wasn't Amy that said it to you, was it?''

''No. Some boy answered when I called and he yelled 'The artist wants to talk to Amy.' Then a girl came to the phone; I'm pretty sure the voice belonged to Carrie Wright—she sounded so glad for a chance to insult me—''

William felt very tired. ''Let's sit outside on the steps and wait for Robert,'' he said. His voice sounded husky even to his own ears.

They sat side by side on the steps watching the light grow brighter in the east. An hour passed and then a part of another one. Once William leaned forward and slept for a few minutes, his head resting on a cushion Sarah had placed on his knees.

Morning had arrived and was full of sunlight when Robert drove up in his truck with Amy in the cab beside him, half-lying against his shoulder with her eyes closed. Sarah and William hurried out to the truck and watched as Robert lifted Amy out of the cab.

"Is she hurt, Robert?" Sarah asked hardly above a whisper.

"Just drunk," Robert answered shortly, "I can't at the moment think of a prettier way to say it—"

He tried to make Amy walk, but when she staggered, he picked her up and carried her to her room upstairs. Then he walked away without a word while Sarah got a basin of cold water and began to bathe Amy's face. William saw and smelled the vomit that covered the front of her dress. She moaned when she turned her head, but she didn't speak or open her eyes.

Sarah turned to William. "She'll be all right—this time. Her body isn't used to alcohol and it's made her sick." She looked out toward the hall where Robert had disappeared. "Go downstairs with Robert. Tell him I'll come down soon and make coffee."

But Robert didn't want any coffee. He said, "I'm going home now. I'll call Sarah later and see how things are."

Then he walked out to his truck and took off down the road in almost as big a hurry as Amy's friend had taken off in his car when they left for the party. Except that Amy's friend was showing off; Robert was mad.

ten

SARAH WAS a long time in coming downstairs, and when she did William noticed that she didn't walk with her usual long stride; her face looked bushed. "Why don't you sleep late this morning?" he asked her. "I'll fix breakfast for the girls when they get up—"

She nodded a thank you and turned right away to go back upstairs. They didn't say a word about what had happened—not even about Robert leaving as he had.

When Carla and Elizabeth came down William filled bowls of fresh fruit for them and made buttered toast. Elizabeth was out of patience with Sarah for sleeping so late. "Sarah knows she s'posed to take us for a walk if she's not painting a picture or working for Mr. Hager," she said grumpily, but she was pacified by William's offer to push each of them in the new swing for a while.

He was too tired to enjoy being with them that morning. Carla was no problem except that she sensed something was wrong in the household and he had to reassure her that everything was all right—that Sarah and Amy were just tired that morning. Elizabeth, however, was more aggressive and demanding, with questions leaping out one after another until William felt his weary brain going into a spin.

"Do you want me to read stories to Elizabeth from my Braille books, William?" Carla asked after a while.

"Would you, Carla?" he answered gratefully. A few minutes later he fell asleep on the porch couch with the soft sound of Carla's voice reading and Elizabeth's excited interruptions sounding in his ears.

He heard Amy come down to the kitchen around noon. She made tea and toast for herself and didn't speak to William until she had finished her breakfast.

She looked at him angrily when she finally spoke. "I suppose Sarah sent Robert out to pick me up last night," she said finally.

"I didn't suppose you knew *who* picked you up," William said quietly. He could see that made her madder than ever. That was all right though; he was mad himself.

"I'll never live this down—" she went on. "I can't even go to a party without having dear old Robert come lumbering up in his work-truck, practically kidnapping me from the party—"

William said, "I'd like to slap you, Amy," and she said, "Well, don't do it, little brother. You might stir up trouble for yourself—"

She went outside, banging the screen door behind her, and started down the path toward the woods. Elizabeth came running after her, curls flying in the breeze. "Wait, Amy—me and Carla want to take a walk with you. Wait—I'll bring Carla—"

"You and Carla stay in the yard, Elizabeth. I don't want either of you with me this morning," Amy said sharply. Elizabeth stopped short in her tracks, looking puzzled and hurt.

Amy came back in midafternoon when Sarah was fixing a snack for all of them. William had just carried trays out under the trees so that Carla and Elizabeth could eat in the cool shade and he walked into the kitchen behind Amy. Sarah looked up from the worktable where she was making a salad.

"Feeling better, Amy?" she asked. Her voice was polite but not friendly.

"Oh, don't be hypocritical, Sarah. You don't care in the least how I feel," Amy snapped.

"That's true. I reproach myself for asking," Sarah answered. Amy was silent for a minute, then she turned on Sarah with a little speech she seemed to have been thinking over.

"No doubt you and Parson Norris have your sermons ready for me, Sarah, but before you climb into the pulpit, I'd like to say a thing or two myself—"

"By all means," Sarah answered. She pushed a kettle off the burner and sitting down in the first chair she found handy, stretched her long legs in front of her looking as if she felt pleasantly lazy, glad to have some conversation with Amy. It was an act, though, William knew; there was a glint in Sarah's eyes.

"I want to say that I'm fed up with things around here," Amy began. "A lot of my friends say I shouldn't be putting up with it, and I'm not going to—"

"Just what aspects of your environment are troubling your friends?" Sarah asked. It was a bookish question and the voice asking the question was full of sarcasm. It probably was intended to make Amy furious, and it did.

"I'll name a few for you, Miss West. For one thing, I don't like being an unpaid baby-sitter for two spoiled brats while you paint your earth-shaking pictures. And more than that, I don't like having nothing of my own, not even a room—"

"You asked to share my room when Mama died. You've never suggested leaving it since. I didn't tie you in it, you know—"

"Well I'm suggesting it now. I don't want to share your room with you—or anything else for that matter. And just for a change, I'd like to live a life of my own without a lot of buttinsky from you or Robert. Sure, I had a few drinks last night, sure I got a little smashed; but after all, who are *you* to lecture me about a little bit of drinking—"

"I don't recall that I've said a word about it so far."

"Oh, you will of course; you'll be rushing out to old Hager with the story in no time. Well, maybe you'd better tell him some stories of your own life. Everybody in town knows your father was a drunk no matter how great you think he was. And everybody certainly knows that you're an unwed mother. I've been humiliated time after time when I've heard that—when I've heard people call Elizabeth a little—"

Amy stopped suddenly and glanced out in the direction of the shade trees where Carla and Elizabeth, finished with their lunch, were rolling in the grass together, laughing uproariously as they rolled across one another and struggled with Nugget who had joined in the romp with them.

For just a few seconds, Amy had nothing more to say. But Sarah did. She said, "Go right ahead, Amy, say it. Don't allow your sensitive nature to hold anything back. Elizabeth is going to have to learn sometime that with people like your friends she'll have to take part of the blame for my mistakes—"

Amy looked ever so slightly ashamed, but not for long. She said, "Well, frankly, I'm sick of this whole set-up. I've been thinking it over and I've decided to move into town with Carrie Wright. She has an apartment and she's going to find a job for me—"

Sarah's eyes were like two black coals in her face. Her voice was hard but not loud when she spoke again. "I hope you and Carrie Wright can lead the good life together, Amy. But remember one thing. Don't come back here flashing tears one minute and dimples the next, expecting to be part of the family again. I haven't the faintest intention of spending the next few years—or months—or even days—of my life wringing my hands in anguish over you. And I'm tough, believe me. When I'm as full of rage as I am right now, I don't dissolve in

131

sweetness and light very soon—actually, not ever—"

Amy didn't answer. She just walked over to the telephone and dialed a number, then very brightly she said, "Can you pick me up this afternoon, Carrie? I'm being tossed out of this happy household on my sweet little ass—" She giggled at something her friend said, then added, "Fine. I'll be ready. I can hardly wait."

William listened as his sister banged dresser drawers upstairs and ran down the long flight when she heard Carrie Wright at the door. They left together, looking as indignant as if Amy were a much abused little girl and Carrie a friend who wasn't for one minute going to put up with that kind of treatment.

It was quiet around the house all afternoon. Elizabeth napped for an hour and then romped with Nugget or played in the swing. Carla followed Sarah from room to room, plainly anxious, but unquestioning, quietly doing whatever Sarah asked her to do without saying a word. When Robert drove out in the late afternoon he sat looking steadily at William, talking about little matters that amounted to almost nothing.

Finally he said, "You'd better tell me, hadn't you?" and William answered just as briefly, "The two of them blew up. She's gone to live with Carrie Wright."

"That's just great," Robert nodded. "Miss Wright will have our little Pine Woods Amy another Carrie in no time flat. As soon as she can handle alcohol, there's—" he cut the rest of his sentence short.

William looked at Robert bleakly. "The family's busted all to pieces now," he said. "I don't know what's going to happen—"

Robert got up without answering. "I have to talk to Sarah," he put his hand on William's shoulder. "She's out back?"

"Yes, with Carla. She's upset. Amy said some of the meanest things you can think of—"

Ordinarily he would have gone with Robert to find Sarah, would have been eager to be with the two of them and join now and then in the conversation. Now he dreaded to hear anything they had to say.

Carla came in a few minutes to sit beside him. "Sarah said maybe you would play with me, William. She has to talk grown-up talk with Robert."

"Sure, Carla. What do you want to play?" he asked.

She turned her small face up to his. "Nothing," she whispered. He put his arm around her and they sat together without saying anything more.

Robert stopped beside them before he left. "I'm going back to town now and see Mr. Hager, William. Maybe he'll know what to do—I hope so anyway." He stooped down and kissed Carla's forehead. "I'll bring my guitar next time, baby, and we'll have another jam session together—"

Carla smiled weakly and nodded. Robert said, "Don't worry, William," and William said, "I'm not so much worried, just kind of sick."

Elizabeth came to sit with them after a while. "Where's Amy, William?" She was not afraid to ask the questions Carla held back.

"She's in town, Elizabeth—staying all night with one of her friends, I guess.

"Is she going to another party?"

"I don't know. I hope not."

"Why did she take all her dresses and things with her?"

"I don't know, Elizabeth. I don't know nothin' about nothin'," he added bitterly.

"You're grumpy, aren't you, William?"

133

"A little. Come on, I'll push you and Carla in the swing—"

"I'm tired of the stupid old swing. I want Amy to come home."

Elizabeth walked away and he could hear her talking to Sarah in the living room, asking questions about Amy.

When it was time for the children to go to bed, Sarah unbuttoned Carla's pinafore out on the porch and then turned to Elizabeth. "I'll get you both ready so you can zip into your night clothes up in your room. I'll be up to tuck you in—"

Elizabeth pulled away from Sarah's hand. "I don't want you to unbutton me or tuck me in—I want Amy," she pouted.

"You know very well that Amy's not here. So unless you want to get all the buttons undone yourself, you'd better stand still—"

The tantrum took over from there. "I *won't* stand still. If Amy can't help me, I'll do all the buttons by myself—" she screamed.

"I'll be glad for you to take over. Go upstairs and help yourself." Sarah sat back in her chair and watched as Elizabeth, screaming at every step, climbed up the stairs.

Carla sighed. "Holy Moses, Sarah," she said, leaning close against Sarah's side.

For the first time that day, Sarah laughed—kind of a sour laugh, yes, but better than nothing. "Holy Moses should be glad he's not around here, shouldn't he, Carla?" She led Carla outside and over to the little orchard to find out if the new oranges were beginning to set on. William joined them. After a while the wails next door quieted down.

Mr. Hager drove out about nine that evening and Mr. Cooper came with him. William wondered if he should leave the living room while they talked, but Sarah said no, and Mr. Hager agreed with her.

"We want to do what is best for your sister, William," he said. "She's going through a stage now that is making it hard for all of us—especially for you and Sarah. But Amy will come through all right; we've just got to help her—" He looked at Sarah as he spoke. She didn't nod or smile. Her face looked frozen.

"If I can persuade Amy to come back, can you accept her and be friends again, Sarah?"

Sarah didn't waste time in answering him. "No, Mr. Hager. I've never cared for the role of martyr; I think it's spineless. If Amy wants to come back here, she can. She has as much right to live here as I do. But if she comes back, I'll leave. And if I leave, I want William and Carla to go with Elizabeth and me."

Mr. Hager shook his head. "No, we can't have that. And we can't have Amy living with that girl the young crowd calls 'the blonde boomerang' either. No little boomerangs of any complexion are going to make Amy indebted to them—"

"If it's the only way left to us, John, Mother and me will take Amy 'til she's through high school—" Mr. Cooper interrupted.

"I hate for you to do that. You and Katy have raised your family—"

"We'll take her. Katy says we will and she's the one to decide."

"I'm afraid it's that or—or something drastic if this goes on."

Sarah spoke suddenly. "Both of you know—so does William—that I was a rebel. I got myself involved in serious trouble. Mary Hand and Mama helped me and so have the two of you—you and your wives. I'm not saying 'holier than thou' to Amy, but I simply can't care for this family and do the work if such episodes as last night's keep up. And I don't intend to take the venom that she spewed out at me this morning—"

"She told me what she said," Mr. Hager said quietly. "She was hysterical, Sarah, scared and guilty. She had to strike out at you, she thought, before either you or Robert struck out at her—"

Sarah nodded, but her face didn't change; the cold, angry look was still there.

"What about you, William? What do you have to say?"

"I just want our family to stick together," William answered. "Amy's walked out on us. I guess the four of us that's left will just have to get along without her—"

Mr. Hager looked at William and then he turned to Mr. Cooper. "Well, let's go now, Ben. Let's go see Katy and talk this situation over—"

When the two men were gone, William turned to Sarah. "Do you think you'll hate her forever, Sarah?" he asked.

She kept looking at him but he had a feeling she wasn't seeing him. When she spoke her voice seemed to wobble the way tired legs wobble after a long day's work.

"I have to get away for a while, William. Right now I'm going to drive the Volksie down to the Gulf and howl at the waves—" She laughed shakily, but there was a look in her face that showed how much she needed to howl. He thought that if it wasn't such a silly thing to do, he'd like to try it himself.

eleven

"A NEW routine soon cuts its own rut," Mr. Cooper said; and after a while William realized those words were true. Within a couple of weeks it no longer seemed quite so strange or hurtful that Amy did not come running down the stairs for breakfast or stand talking away at the rate of a mile a minute while she helped Sarah cook a meal. They all missed Amy—Sarah must have, although she didn't say a word. The little girls were puzzled at first, and anxious, asking a hundred questions that had to be dodged or smoothed over. William, perhaps, missed her most of all. There had been an Amy around all his life; he began to understand how close they'd been to one another in spite of the fights and mad words they'd tossed around.

He went over to the Coopers to see her occasionally and they talked, but not in the free way they did once. On one of these visits Amy said, "I'm ashamed, yes, but that's it. I've told that to Mr. Hager once, and I won't say anything about it again—" William thought, well, you couldn't blame her; you can't go around beating yourself over the head for something that's over and done. And it was certainly over and done. It seemed like Amy had smashed something that morning when she came in from her walk and lit in on Sarah—something thin and precious like Mary Hand's crystal, which they kept locked up in the dining room cabinet.

Mr. Cooper came over one morning and talked about Amy, although Sarah hadn't asked a word about her. "She's doin' fine, Sarah; I thought you'd want to know. Amy's a good girl except for these flare-ups now and then—she'll get over them as she grows up. Right now she'd do anything you'd ask if only she could come back to her family—" He looked at Sarah like maybe he was begging a favor.

William had seen Sarah angry any number of times, but she usually blew up and then things settled back to normal. Not now. Her face and voice were so cold that even Mr. Cooper looked away and seemed sorry that he'd said anything about Amy in the first place.

"Amy can come back any time she pleases, Mr. Cooper, but not to the children and me. If she wants to come back, that's all right, but I will leave and take the children with me. I tried to make you and Mr. Hager understand that—"

Mr. Cooper was thoughtful for a while. "It's not that we mind keepin' her, Sarah. She helps Mother with lots of things and she's just as nice a little lady as you please. I know you and her was fond of one another not so long ago—"

"That's right. I feel a great loss, Mr. Cooper, the kind of loss that can't be replaced—"

There was a great change in Sarah during the next few weeks. She was quieter than she used to be—apt to go away by herself with a book when she had some free time, or occasionally to leave in the Volkswagen without inviting either William or Carla and Elizabeth to go along. She put her painting materials away shortly after Amy left, and William heard her refusing orders to do pictures when people called her on the phone. Sometimes when he tried to talk to her it seemed as if she'd pulled a mask over her face.

Then suddenly neither Amy's break with the family nor the change in Sarah was important. The emphasis was all on Carla after the day Dr. Finley asked William and Sarah to come to his office to talk with him and Mr. Hager.

"Carla was born with cataracts on her eyes," Dr. Finley told them as soon as they were seated. "I am not an ophthalmologist. I haven't been sure, but I talked with Bill Saunders about the possibility of cataracts, and he was trying to find money to take her to a clinic in Atlanta when he was laid off work for several months the year Carla was two. Then there was the accident shortly after he'd been called back on the job. After that there were money problems for Libby and finally her long illness—" Dr. Finley's face looked sad. "Carla has been caught up in a whole series of tragedies. One of the worst is that she should have had surgery a long time ago—"

"Is there any hope that surgery can help her now, Dr. Finley?" Sarah asked in a low voice.

"That's what I want to talk to you and William about. I was in Boston last week at a medical meeting and I had a long conversation with an old friend of mine. He is Dr. Carl Zitek—nationally known for his work in eye surgery, especially known for his work with children. I told him about Carla and he agreed with me that we should bring her to Boston and let him determine whether or not her eyes warrant surgery. Since she's only eight, he thinks there is a chance that if the eyes have been stimulated under the cataracts, he may be able to restore her sight—"

"You think the retinas of her eyes have been stimulated, don't you, Dr. Finley?" Mr. Hager asked.

"I'm sure of it. She can distinguish between light and darkness, she can detect movement and form—"

William's heart was pounding and his face must have shown the turmoil inside him for Dr. Finley turned and spoke to him directly.

"We might get the operation done more cheaply closer home, William, but I think you'll agree with me that your little sister must have the best. I feel very strongly that Carl Zitek must do this surgery—"

"But she's never been away from home—or us—Dr. Finley," William exclaimed. "She would be so scared—by herself in a strange place—"

"Yes—" Dr. Finley turned toward Sarah with a smile that looked as if it apologized for something. "I'm afraid, Sarah, that we're going to have to ask you to take Libby's place once more. You'll have to go with Carla, stay by her side night and day until Zitek can calm her fears. After surgery you must be there to see that she is absolutely quiet; she could damage her eyes terribly if she should get agitated—"

Sarah had placed her hands against her temples as William had often seen her do when things were getting out of hand.

"I'm about to do a crash landing, Dr. Finley. I'm thinking of what I'd do about Elizabeth, about the garden, about finding money for this trip and surgery—" she turned to look at Mr. Hager. "About my job—"

"Let's take one thing at a time," Dr. Finley said gently. "I know there's been some trouble with Amy, but don't you think she might come home and take care of Elizabeth in this emergency?"

William saw Sarah stiffen; he also saw Mr. Hager shake his head slightly as he looked at Dr. Finley.

"Don't worry about your job, Sarah," Mr. Hager said. "My daughter will come in and help me out while you're gone, just as she did after Libby got too ill for work. As for Little Britches, Clare and I talked about her as soon as Dr. Finley told me about the possibility of this trip to Boston. Clare wants to keep Elizabeth while you're gone—in fact, she's eager to do it. As for the garden, there sits an able young man who will have help from Ben Cooper and Robert Norris—"

"Yes," William said quietly, "I can take care of things. I know I can—"

"As for money," Dr. Finley interrupted, "you'll have help. I intend to speak to different groups here in town. We'll ask *The News* to run special articles. People in a small town like this are pretty generous when a blind child is the center of a problem—"

"I'll paint," Sarah said in a determined voice. "I've been reneging lately—but I'll get at it again. If you know of anybody who wants a painting of a French poodle or Siamese cat—or—" she smiled at William—"a palomino colt—"

"I'll tell them that you'll do it for them," Dr. Finley said, "but I'll warn them that it won't be done for a song. If they want an original Sarah West painting, they're going to have to pay for it."

William and Sarah drove home in a daze after the interview with Dr. Finley was over. As they drew near the house, Sarah turned to him.

"A whole new world is opening to us, William. I'm happy and hopeful—and scared to be either happy or hopeful—"

"I'm more happy than scared," William answered. "I have a gut-feeling that things are going to turn out right—"

She smiled at him. He realized that she knew he'd borrowed the words "gut-feeling" from times when she'd tried to explain that she was satisfied with one of her pictures—she'd had that kind of feeling about it.

When he told Amy about their plans the next day, there were tears. "Oh, William, I want to be a part of the family again," she said when she was able to talk. "I'll lose my mind if Sarah doesn't let me come home

141

and help her get Carla ready for this trip to Boston—"

"I want you back too, Amy. We really need you—but—" he broke off speaking. There was no use trying to pretend that maybe Sarah would relent. He had seen the look on her face when Dr. Finley mentioned Amy.

"Sarah has no right to push me out like this. Carla's *my* little sister—"

He was sorry for Amy and suddenly angry at the same time. "That's right," he said, "and she was your little sister the day you walked out on all of us and said things you knew would hurt Sarah. They hurt her, all right. Robert knows that—"

She just sat and looked at him. Finally she said, "You know how to say hurtful things, too, William."

The fund for Carla began to grow as soon as word spread around town about the surgery needed to give a little girl the sight she had never known. Dr. Finley spoke to the Lions Club and immediately several hundred dollars poured in. Mr. Hager talked to church groups and again the donations swelled the fund established especially for Carla.

There were small donations from nurses down at the hospital who remembered when Carla was born, there were some from the children who attended Carla's school, and others from teachers at the public schools who had known both Amy and William.

Each week that summer when Robert paid William for his work he added another ten dollars for what they had come to call the "Carla Fund." Amy had been able to get a job during vacation at the new cafeteria which opened in town that spring. After work she washed cars and every few days she handed her earnings to William without saying a word. At first when he gave the money to Sarah, he told her—half-hoping that she might soften and send a word of thanks—that Amy was sending it for Carla's operation. But she didn't. She'd just say, "Please ask Mr. Hager to deposit this in Carla's fund" —and her face had the same closed look it wore every time Amy's name was mentioned.

William could hardly believe the number of people ready to help send Carla to Boston and the surgeon Dr. Finley trusted. Once a man whom none of them knew won a hundred dollars in a poker game and he took it to the newspaper asking the people there to see that it got to that "little blind kid out in the Pine Woods development."

One week the newspaper printed a story about Sarah—careful, of course, to mention that she was the daughter of Jason West—and telling all about her living back in a relative's old home, caring for her own child and three orphaned children next door. At the end, the article got around to talk of the effort being made by various townspeople to raise funds for surgery on a little eight-year-old girl's eyes.

That article brought a number of small donations to the Carla Fund, but it had a farther-reaching effect which no one anticipated.

One of the national magazines spotted the story and called to ask if they could send out a reporter to do a story about Jason West, his daughter, and the children she was caring for.

"Aren't you thrilled, Sarah?" Mrs. Hager asked when she came out one evening, and Sarah said that she'd be considerably more thrilled to see a good rain waking up their potato crop.

But when she was told what the magazine would pay for the article, she was thoughtful.

"I hate the idea," she told William, "the very thought

of someone delving into my life makes me furious. Still—" she sat thinking for a while and then she said, "that money would give Carla's fund a big lift."

The magazine sent down a young lady named Tracy Gregg who was as pretty and bouncy as Amy used to be when everything was going right for her. She spent three days with them and though you would have thought she was just down for a holiday, William guessed that she wasn't missing a trick. She was curious about Amy. "When will I get to see that beautiful girl in the portrait above the fireplace?" she wanted to know. Sarah told her that Amy was staying with neighbors for the summer—"nearer town where she has a job" was the reason she gave—but it sounded like a flabby excuse even to William, and he could see a suspicious look in Tracy Gregg's eyes. It didn't matter though; Tracy was more interested in hearing about Sarah's father and her childhood, in hearing about Mama and how Sarah had come to take care of the children next door. She talked to Sarah about painting and took pictures of the portraits hanging in the living room. "These will introduce the children and at the same time exhibit a phase of your art," she told Sarah.

Sometimes when Tracy Gregg took a walk in the woods with William and Elizabeth and Carla, she would ask William an occasional question, carelessly as if the answer didn't really matter, but William was wary. He was old enough to understand that the stories of her father's drinking were painful for Sarah—she had never talked about them with anyone except William. He remembered how she had cut Amy off the morning his sister brought up the subject of Elizabeth's father. He guessed, too, that family quarrels were not to be aired in a magazine.

He *did* talk to Tracy though about the thinking stone

that Papa had pointed out to him long ago; he told her what the hurricane was like and the hard work needed to clear up after it. One day he told her how they used to walk into town with William pulling the little girls in his old wagon while Sarah held a purple parasol over them, how some adolescents made fun of them, and Amy didn't like being a part of the family when they all went into town together. Tracy Gregg smiled at the things he told her. "I'll make a note of all this," she said. "Little tidbits like these will give color to my story."

One day she asked about Amy. "I imagine Sarah and Amy are good friends, aren't they? They're not so very far apart in age—and Sarah painted that beautiful portrait of Amy—"

William knew her words were meant to sound careless, but he answered her very carefully. "We're a family," he told her. "We have our ups and downs—"

When the magazine accepted Tracy's story, Sarah received a check that sent Carla's fund leaping high. About that time Mary Hand sent her Social Security check for the month of Carla's birthday and Sarah finished a mural she had suggested doing when a lady in town wanted portraits painted of her five grandchildren, aged two years to eight.

In a wide panel which was to hang above the lady's fireplace Sarah sketched the five children at play on a grassy slope with trees and flowers around them, with a few white clouds above and the gold of sunlight all around them. The oldest girl held the youngest one on her lap and was showing him pictures in an open book; a small boy and girl were dressing a kitten in a bonnet and shawl; an older eight-year-old boy sat hugging his knees and staring soberly at something in the distance. The lady liked the sketch a lot and so Sarah eagerly began work on it.

William was working with Robert Norris six days a week during the summer vacation, but while Sarah was doing the mural he took Saturdays off so that he could tend the garden and do the cooking while she took advantage of every hour of light she could use for her painting. His cooking wasn't the best in the world; Elizabeth let him know that. "You sure do like scrambled eggs and peanut butter sandwiches, don't you, William?" she asked wearily when William offered her and Carla the same food three days running.

Sometimes, though, Robert brought hamburgers from a café in town and occasionally a carton of ice cream for a treat. That made supper a big affair, something like a party. Robert usually played his guitar after they were through eating, and all of them sat out in the yard and sang. Mrs. Cooper told William that Amy cried when she heard them singing.

Many people in town liked the mural when Sarah finished it. William stood looking at it for a long time before she wrapped it for delivery.

"They look like little kids in a book of fairy tales," he told Sarah, and she nodded. "That's what I tried to do—a never-never land effect with the faces of real children." She smiled to herself. "It must be pretty good, William. My reason for thinking so is that I'd like so much to show it to Jason—"

One day Sarah handed over a delicate and difficult task to William. "I think you're the one to explain things to Carla," she said, looking at him thoughtfully. "She loves and trusts you, perhaps more than any of us; I believe it will be less frightening to her if you tell her about Boston than if either Dr. Finley or I do—"

Carla had grown quieter as the years passed; she still liked to sing when Robert played his guitar, she still romped with Elizabeth and the dogs, but she was not the chatterbox she had been at four. Sometimes she liked to draw away from everyone and read her Braille books or listen by the hour to records Sarah bought for her to play on Mary Hand's old phonograph. It wasn't, William thought, that Carla was sad, but that there was something secret and delicate about her—something you'd hate terribly to hurt.

That dread of hurting her increased during the first few minutes of trying to explain how they hoped to help her, of watching the bewilderment and then something like terror coming into her face. A place called Boston, a doctor who was not Dr. Finley, something strange and frightening done to her eyes—Carla began to tremble and William felt weak for fear he was not saying the right things.

"Sarah will stay with you every minute, Carla, and Dr. Finley says this surgeon in Boston is very kind to little girls like you. You'll never feel any hurt at all, and if you're brave and do what this doctor tells you to do—we're not absolutely sure, Carla, but we think maybe you'll be able to see—"

"What's it like to see?" she asked when her first trembling grew quieter.

He struggled for an answer. "You'll see more with your eyes than you ever have with your hands, Carla. Your hands tell you that Elizabeth's hair is soft and curly, but your eyes will tell you that it's bright gold. They will tell you that Nugget is gold too, a little like Elizabeth's hair—"

"And if the doctor can't make me see, will I be just the way I am now?"

"Yes," he said, the tightness in his throat hurting.

"That's all right. I like the way I've always been."

"But you'll go with Sarah, won't you?"

"Yes. If you're sure Sarah won't leave me."

"She wouldn't leave you. Nothing could ever make Sarah leave you."

Carla drew a deep breath. "I'm scared," she whispered. "I'm real scared, William." Then when she found her voice she added, "But no matter how scared I am, I won't cry—and maybe when I come back, I'll see Elizabeth's hair and Nugget—and you." She touched his face with her hands and he noticed that they were cold.

That night Carla slept in Amy's bed next to Sarah. Standing in the hall, William heard her talking long after she should have been asleep.

"We'll stay together every minute, won't we, Sarah?"

"Yes. Even when you're asleep I'll be in a bed next to you so that you'll never be afraid when you wake up—"

"We'll stay *very* close together, won't we, Sarah?"

"Yes. *Very* close together."

"Like we was Mama and Carla, won't we?"

"Yes, like that," Sarah answered.

The next few days were full of preparation for the trip to Boston, for risking three thousand dollars that Carla would be able to see. Everyone tried to amuse her, hoping to keep her from feeling frightened, but it was not an easy thing to do.

Once as William walked with her down the woods road and tried to tell her something very funny that Johnny Hager had done in school, Carla interrupted him very quietly. "I don't know if I *want* to see things, William. Seems I'd like better just to stay home and be the way I am now—"

On the day of departure Carla went over to the Coopers with William to say good-bye to them and to Amy. It was not an easy time; Carla was the bravest of all of them. She stood straight and slender as a little tree, her sightless eyes turned up to them as she held tightly to Amy's hand.

"You don't have to worry—I'm not going to cry," she said. "I promised Sarah and Robert when we talked about it. I'm going to be braver than a lot of kids older than I am—"

William noticed though, that there were tears on Carla's cheeks when he leaned into the window of the Volkswagen to say good-bye before Robert drove her and Sarah to the airport.

William went over and stayed with Amy for the rest of the afternoon. When they saw Robert turn the Volksie into Mary Hand's drive on his return from the airport, they ran over to meet him.

"It was pretty bad," Robert said slowly. "We tried to amuse her at the airport. I bought a velvet kitten for her to hold on the flight, but she wouldn't say a word—just smiled when we tried to be funny and that was all. Then when she realized that they were boarding the plane, she began to cry, screaming to Sarah that she wanted to go back home, that she didn't want to see. I had to carry her on the plane."

William turned away from Robert and Amy, and walked off into the woods. He couldn't ever remember needing to be alone so much.

twelve

ELIZABETH WAS not happy at being away from home. "But Mrs. Hager is so nice to you, Elizabeth," Amy told her when she and William drove over with Robert that evening to see how the youngest member of their family was doing.

"I know she is so nice, Amy, but I want to be with you and William," Elizabeth said firmly.

"She'll be fine by tomorrow," Mr. Hager promised. William had silent doubts about that.

Mr. Hager put in a call to the hospital in Boston early in the evening. It seemed forever until Sarah was located; then Amy and William took turns at listening on the extension in Mr. Hager's study.

"She's asleep now." Sarah's voice sounded tired. "The nurse gave her a sedative when we got here. I have a cot beside her—" There was a pause, then "How is my girl doing?" she asked.

Mr. Hager said that Elizabeth was going to be fine. Then Sarah added, "Tell William everything's going to be all right, and thank Robert again for me. I don't know what I'd have done without him at the airport—"

The conversation went on for a minute or more. There wasn't a word from Sarah to Amy. William took his sister's hand as they walked down the path to Robert's truck.

The next evening they drove in to see if Elizabeth was contented. She wasn't and the Hagers looked worried.

"She says there's a nest of baby tigers in the woods," Mrs. Hager began.

"There is," Elizabeth interrupted. "And their mother went away. They'll die if I don't take care of them."

Then Mr. Hager, in his sternest lawyer voice, took over. "Now listen, Elizabeth, is there any reason why William can't take care of them?" he asked.

"William doesn't know where they are."

"Well, can't you tell him *about* where they are so he can go out and find them?"

William had seen Elizabeth cornered before in some of her imagined stories. She had never liked the experience, and she didn't like it now.

"Please don't say so many questions, Mr. Hager. Your chatter makes my head ache," she told him, her large blue eyes looking as cool as Sarah's did sometimes.

Mr. Hager went to stand looking out the window and they could see his shoulders shaking slightly. After a while he turned and asked William and Amy into his study while Robert held Elizabeth and talked to Mrs. Hager. "I think I'll let her go to the Coopers with you tonight, Amy. She cried for over an hour last night—the poor little tyke's lonesome for some of her family. But bring her with you of a morning when you come into town for your day's work. We can't put too much of a burden on Katy Cooper."

And so each evening Robert and William picked Amy up after her work at the cafeteria was done, then stopped at the Hagers' for Elizabeth who would come tearing down the steps to throw her arms around Amy. "Maybe if Sarah saw *that* someday," Robert said quietly to William as they walked a short distance behind the girls to his truck, "maybe that would make a difference—"

William shook his head. "I don't think it would matter," he said, "I don't think Sarah's ever going to be friends with Amy again."

News came from Boston in bits and pieces—some-

times a report from the doctor that sent their spirits up-
ward, sometimes a note that Sarah sent to William just to
cheer him and ease his loneliness. One such note read:

"Carla is content now, and shows no sign of fear or anxi-
ety. The nurses have made her a special pet and she thinks
she may marry Dr. Zitek. He tells her that he'll speak to his
wife and seven grandchildren about it. He is marvelous
with children—has won Carla's confidence completely."

The report they had hoped for, and dreaded at the
same time, came by way of a telephone call from Sarah to
Mr. Hager. The doctor had operated on Carla's eyes that
morning and had found them to be normal under the
cataracts. Sarah would have to stay near her, keep her
quiet and contented for the next ten days while the eyes
healed.

William went out to his thinking stone that evening
after the news of the telephone call had been relayed to
him. A long time ago his father had told him that a
thinking stone was a place to think not only when things
were troubling but also in times when one wanted to say
"Praise the Lord."

"This is that kind of time," he thought, and he sat for
an hour on the old froglike boulder, just being thankful.

In spite of the good news from Boston, Amy grew
sadder as the days passed. She would come over to Mary
Hand's house sometimes to do a bit of cleaning, and
she looked around as if each familiar object she polished
or dusted was something that hurt her, something
that was likely to start tears.

She stood in the middle of the living room and
looked around as if she had forgotten the friendly old
room with the worn carpet, Sarah's pictures on the walls,

the little girls' rocking chairs brought in from the porch to keep them safe from the weather.

"I feel as if I'd been gone for years," she told William. "I don't feel I belong here anymore." She sat down on the couch suddenly and looked up at him. There was an earnestness about her that made him uneasy.

"I'm scared, William. I'm afraid Carla is going to be closer to Sarah than she is to me. She'll have her sight, but she won't be my little sister—"

"Don't be a fool." William's words and tone were much more brusque than he felt. "You know very well that Carla loves you—she always has—"

"I know very well that Sarah is more important to Carla these days than anyone else. Carla may feel that way for the rest of her life—"

Amy hid her face in her hands and she was still sitting that way when William walked out of the room.

A few days later he received another letter from Sarah:

"They fitted glasses on Carla this morning and, William, *she can see!* She looked up at me so bewildered and wondering until I spoke to her and then she said, 'Oh, so that's the way you are, Sarah.' She made me sit beside her for a long time so that her hands could compare the face she's known through touch with the one she was seeing for the first time.

"Tell Robert about this, William, and the Hagers and Dr. Finley. Tell the Coopers and make Elizabeth understand the wonderful thing that has happened to her sister—"

William read the letter again and then stood looking at it thoughtfully. He decided to tell Amy that Carla had been fitted with glasses, that she could see and was very happy. The entire letter was not one, he thought, that Amy should read right now.

After the first few days of healing, Carla's eyes were well enough so that she could be moved from the hospital. But Carla must stay in Boston, the doctor told Sarah, until he was sure that all was going well. Sarah wrote about their days of waiting:

"I've found a tiny bedroom in a rooming house near the hospital and Carla and I have moved in. We take long walks and soak up this bland sunlight while we talk about things at home. We wonder if William and Blue Streak have time for a gallop after school before William has to begin planting next year's garden; we wonder how Robert's new landscaping business is coming along; we wonder if Elizabeth and the dogs will be as glad to see us as we will be to see them. We're homesick, William, there's no doubt about that, but we're so happy that the home-sickness doesn't matter much—"

Finally they came home in late November. On the day before they were to arrive, Amy came over to talk with Robert and William when they drove in from town.

"I'm going to cook supper over here tomorrow night," she said firmly. "I don't know whether Sarah will speak to me or not—" she paused and looked up at Robert with troubled eyes, "but I'm going to cook supper for you and the Coopers and my family. What is most important, I'm going to be here and see Carla when the rest of you see her—"

That was the moment William would remember with deep satisfaction. Robert went over and took Amy in his arms. They stood together and when Amy cried, Robert kissed her.

"That's the way I've always wanted it," William thought as he walked away and left them alone. He went down to the pasture gate and talked to the palomino while he stroked its face. "She'll be safe with Robert," he told Blue Streak. "I hope they'll get married—I wish they'd get married tomorrow."

Robert drove to the airport the next afternoon to meet the homecomers while Amy worked to prepare the best supper she knew how to cook. Elizabeth darted about, full of excitement; and as he helped his sister with every chore she set for him, William was wondering, hoping, and dreading the time when Sarah and Amy would meet again after all the months of avoiding one another.

The three of them gathered great armfuls of flowers and bright leaves for the bowls in the living room and a centerpiece for the table. Amy found candles stored away against the threat of hurricanes, and she set them in clusters near the centerpiece and at either end of the table. Then she lighted every candle and let them burn for a minute so that William and Elizabeth could see how beautiful the table would look for Carla that night.

Carla walked up the front steps at twilight, slowly and carefully, but spurning Robert's protective hand held out to her. Amy had kept the lights in the living room dimmed to be sure they didn't hurt the newly restored eyes, and the three of them—Amy, Elizabeth and William—stood back almost shyly as if some stranger were coming to visit them.

There was a difference in Carla—William noticed it immediately. It was not just the unfamiliar glasses or the brown eyes that glowed with life—it was something joyous about her as if a caged little girl had lately been set free.

She laughed as she ran to Elizabeth and then to William, first hugging and then standing back to look at them. "You're like what my fingers used to tell me about you," she said, "only you're nicer—a lot, lot nicer—"

She stood before the two of them so long that William begged her in his thoughts, Please go to Amy. It will kill Amy if you don't go to her, Carla—

Suddenly she did. She looked up and stared at the tall girl standing to one side. At first Carla seemed bewildered and then a look of understanding came into her eyes. She said, "Oh, you're Amy—you're my Amy—" Then she ran into Amy's arms and threw herself against her sister's body. They stayed like that for what seemed a long time. Mr. Cooper wiped his eyes; William felt like crying, but he didn't. Sarah looked down at Nugget who was trying to get her attention. Her face had no expression in it.

At supper neither Sarah nor Amy ate very much. So far as William knew they had only greeted one another briefly and hadn't spoke since. In the excitement over Carla, he had hardly had time to say more than a few words to Sarah; at the table he looked at her steadily until she smiled at him—not a very happy smile—and he wondered drearily if she were angry or disappointed in him. She had looked surprised when Mrs. Cooper told her how Elizabeth's homesickness had led Mr. Hager to allow her to spend the nights with Amy and only the days with the Hagers. And earlier when Elizabeth had squealed, "Wait 'til you see the beautiful table and the good things Amy has cooked for supper," Sarah had said nothing, just took Elizabeth's hand, and held it against her cheek for a few seconds.

Halfway through the meal, Carla leaned back in her chair and closed her eyes. "I have to go back to other times for a while," she said, weariness showing in her face. "I have to rest my seeing until it gets used to all of you—"

They gathered in the living room after supper to rest

after the excitement and emotion of earlier hours. Carla leaned against Robert, who sat on the couch beside Sarah. Elizabeth ran to climb up on Sarah's lap.

"You feel so good, Sarah," she said, looking up into her mother's face. "Your lap feels good like in the olden times when I was just a little girl—"

Sarah smiled down at her. She seemed to grope for something to say. "Your new dress is pretty, Elizabeth," she remarked finally. "Did Mrs. Hager make it for you?"

"No. Amy did. And she let me wear it tonight so that I would look nice and Carla wouldn't be disappointed—" She stretched across the space between them to touch Carla's cheek. "You didn't be disappointed when you saw me, did you, Carla?"

Carla roused herself and scooted over, taking Elizabeth's small, fat hand in hers. She laughed and the two girls rubbed noses as Mr. Cooper had taught them to do when Elizabeth was not more than two years old. "Two little Florida crackers turned Eskimo," he used to call them.

"I wasn't disappointed, Elizabeth," Carla told her. "I think you're as beautiful as Sarah and Amy—"

"Have you showed Sarah the picture you made for her?" Robert asked after a while, and Elizabeth slipped like an eel from Sarah's lap to run upstairs and find the picture. When she came back carrying a square of cardboard filled with crayon drawings, she held it up in front of Sarah.

"It's for you, Sarah. Robert bought crayons for me and Amy showed me how to stay inside the lines she made for me, but *I'm* the artist—" She pranced with impatience. "Hurry up and say it, Sarah. Do you like it?"

"I like it very much, Elizabeth," Sarah said quietly. "Nice colors—very, very nice—"

"Do you know what it is?" Elizabeth asked.

"I was wondering. A flower bed, maybe? Or a sunset?"

Elizabeth looked disgusted. "No, silly. It's a bowl of salad Mrs. Hager made one day—see, red tomatoes, white cauliflower, green lettuce. Here's green peppers—I had to push the crayon hard for these peppers—" She held her work at arm's length and looked proudly at it. "You can see what all these colors mean now, can't you, Sarah?"

"Of course. Stupid of me not to recognize it."

"Amy likes it a lot. She told me there was an artist that would be my grandpa if he didn't die, and Amy said he'd be so proud of me—"

William saw Sarah's glance go quickly to Amy's face. Sarah didn't smile, just looked surprised, and for a few seconds she seemed to be thinking carefully.

Elizabeth brought her attention back to the picture in a hurry. "You can hang it in your room, Sarah. Then when Amy comes home again, both of you can look at it—" She took the cardboard from Sarah's hand and gave it to Carla. "Look, Carla, now that the doctor in Boston made you see, I can show you how to color. Then you can be an artist like me—"

Carla shook her head. "No, Elizabeth, I think I'm going to be a singer. And I'm going to have big boys like Robert playing guitars beside me so the music will make my singing prettier."

All at once Sarah's face lighted up. She turned toward Amy who sat across the room and laughed a low quiet laugh the way she used to.

"It looks, Amy, as if our girls are both leaning toward the arts," she said, and Amy nodded, then closed her eyes for just a second. Amy looked, William thought, as if she'd traveled a long way.

thirteen

AMY CAME home and it was just as if she'd never been away so far as Carla and Elizabeth were concerned. No excitement, no fuss, no tears—just the whole family sleeping in Mary Hand's house again, everybody piling into the Volksie to ride into town to school or work, all of them having blueberry muffins for Sunday breakfast once again.

It was not quite the same for the three older members of the family. Mostly, William was full of relief that they were all together once more and at peace; sometimes, though, he got anxious when it looked as if moods might be getting deeper, remarks so rigidly polite that one had the feeling two uncomfortable strangers had been forced to live together and keep up the appearance of liking one another.

There was no mention of sharing the same room as Sarah and Amy had gladly done to find comfort in being with one another the night after Mama's funeral.

"Would you like the room opposite William's, Amy?" Sarah had asked carelessly. "It has the chintz draperies you always liked—"

Amy nodded. Her face showed plainly enough that she remembered things that had been said on an afternoon when she left with Carrie Wright.

Occasionally the girls had a long talk—William heard them sometimes talking for hours in Amy's room and he was encouraged. If they were still on the outs, he thought, they wouldn't make it a point to talk together.

When he had the opportunity, he asked Amy about those sessions with Sarah, and she answered him without the sauciness she used to show whenever he asked her a question.

"We have to get the air cleared between us," Amy answered slowly. "There are a lot of hate spots in both of us—we each know they're inside us—and we know why. I can't blame Sarah when I remember the things I said to her the day I left; and she knows she was tough with me when I was alone over at the Coopers and worried about Carla—" Amy turned toward her brother, smiling. "Things are relaxing a little. We are able to laugh once in a while."

There was one interest both the older girls and William shared—that was in watching Carla gain confidence in her surroundings, in helping her to understand the world she had known only by touch and sound.

"I want to see William climb up high in the orange trees," Carla said one morning shortly after her return. "I want to see where Mr. Cooper sells vegetables—and all the rooms in the house where we used to live with Mama."

One day Amy gathered up a pile of snapshots. Some were of Mama alone—two or three of her and Papa when they were young. Many were of Mama holding a baby who was either Amy or William or Carla. Amy and William sat beside Carla, and Amy told her what she could remember about each picture.

William hoped some of the pictures would make Carla laugh—one of him as a baby splashing in the bathtub, one of Amy when she was five or six and dressed like a witch for Halloween. But Carla didn't smile at any of the pictures. She would look at each one of them gravely, then putting the pack in order, begin to go through them again.

"Can I keep them?" she asked Amy. "When I'm big

I'll put them in frames and hang them in my room."

Mr. Hager agreed with Sarah and Amy that Carla should not be enrolled in school until she had time to adjust to books and the experience of learning to read with her eyes rather than her fingers. She liked for William to sit beside her and read the books they'd either bought or borrowed from the library in town. She was quick to recognize words under pictures in her storybooks and she read them to Elizabeth with pride.

"Now read me a story with your fingers the way you used to do, Carla," Elizabeth said one day, for that skill of Carla's seemed particularly wonderful to her—it was something that neither the big girls nor William could do.

But Carla wouldn't. She put her Braille books far down under stacks of paint boxes and storybooks where they couldn't be seen. One day she asked William to take them back to her old school.

"Give them to the other kids," she said. "They can read them until some day when they can have surgery." "Surgery" had become a beautiful word to Carla.

Carla had a letter from Mary Hand at Christmas. "The best gift any of us have had this year is the wonderful thing surgery has done for our Carla," it said in part. "I'm coming down in a few weeks to get acquainted with Elizabeth and to see your beautiful new eyes—"

It was the first letter Carla had ever had addressed to herself alone. Amy had to read it to her, but Carla put it away with her snapshots of Mama and waited for the time when she could read it herself.

Mary Hand came down in mid-January, just as the family was getting the spring garden planted. Her aged father had died in his sleep that fall, and Mary, after years of caring for him, wanted to be in her childhood home once more. "I need to have young people around me again," she wrote. "It will do me good to be with you children—"

She was almost the same Mary Hand William remembered from his early childhood—not quite, but almost. She moved a little more slowly and she didn't hear quite so well, but her voice was the same—raspy but nice; and when they talked, she smiled at William in a way that made him almost sure she loved him.

Carla had a dim memory of Mary Hand, but Elizabeth looked at her curiously and was cagey at first about allowing herself to be coaxed to sit on Mary Hand's lap. But as she listened to stories of the days when Amy was a baby and had lived with Mary for months, Elizabeth smiled and grew friendlier.

"You look a lot like your mother, young lady," Mary Hand told her, smoothing Elizabeth's hair back from her temples.

"Amy says I look like Sarah," Elizabeth answered.

"Well, isn't Sarah your mother?" Mary Hand asked.

"Oh, I don't know—I guess so. Mostly though, she's just Sarah."

Mary Hand thought about that for a little while. "Well, anyway, you have the same Jason West look in your eyes that Sarah used to have when she was your age—"

Carla led their guest on a tour of the house to see how three weeks of housecleaning had made it bright and ready for company.

"It looked pretty crumby, and we didn't want you to see it that way," Carla explained. "Robert painted the kitchen and William helped Sarah wash the windows— we tried real hard to make things nice for you," she said leading Mary Hand to the room Amy had prepared for her. "See—Amy fixed this bowl of flowers to make you feel good on your first night here—"

That evening after supper William took his turn in showing Mary Hand around. She was interested in the truck garden with all the small new plants looking green and healthy and at the flats of flowers Robert had brought out for Amy to plant in the yard; but the sight of the empty house next door made her sad.

"It was a pretty little house, William; your papa was a proud young man when he brought his new wife out to see it. We all worked on it together—your folks and I; we planted new shrubs that year and papered the rooms the way Mama wanted them. We used to call it a storybook house because it was so little; but then the family began growing and more rooms and screened porches had to be added—" William noticed that Mary's faded eyes were full of tears. "It hurts me to see it going to ruin like this," she added.

"I think Robert's going to fix it up as soon as he can. He told me that he has to make some plans with Mr. Hager about buying it from Amy and Carla and me— we're minors, you know," he explained, not sure that she would understand Robert's legal problems.

She looked at him sharply. "Why on earth would Robert want to buy this place?" she asked. She suddenly seemed almost angry with Robert, though earlier she'd made a fuss over him when he came to see her at suppertime. "Is Robert getting married?" she asked.

"He hasn't exactly told me—I don't know too much about his plans—" William answered carefully.

Robert took Amy to see a movie that evening. Mary Hand had been looking troubled after she and William came in from their walk, and Amy noticed it. She kissed Mary before they left. "We'll be back early. If you're not asleep, can I come in and talk the way we used to do? I've got so many things to tell you—"

When they were gone, Mary Hand turned to Sarah. "Those children are serious, aren't they, Sarah?"

Sarah smiled. "You pick up cues, Mary Hand," she said.

"Do you approve?"

"It wouldn't make the slightest difference whether I approved or not. But I do. I approve wholeheartedly. So does William."

"William's still a child," Mary Hand said brusquely as if William weren't within hearing distance.

"Twelve-year-olds are sometimes more knowledgeable than you might guess," Sarah said quietly.

"She's too young to be getting serious about Robert. She's hardly more than a little girl—"

"She's seventeen. Juliet was only fourteen when the great love affair of the centuries began—"

"You sound just like Jason, Sarah—" Mary sat looking at Sarah thoughtfully for a while, then she turned to William.

"Well, what do you think of your sister getting married, young man, since you're such a knowledgeable twelve-year-old?"

"I think she needs somebody like Robert to keep her steady. Amy's a little flighty sometimes."

Mary Hand frowned at him. "Amy seems to me to be a very capable young woman, William. I don't find her flighty at all—"

"She is, though," William answered in a firm voice.

Mary Hand looked at him severely. "Insecure, William—not flighty."

She and Amy talked a long time that night—Heaven only knew what about—and the next day Mary went into town to talk with Mr. Hager. That night she gathered all of them, including Robert, into the living room and told them that she had decided to approve the wedding, provided it was delayed until Amy was through high school. "So now, we'll say no more about it," she said grandly, and went outside to watch Elizabeth and Carla playing in the yard.

There were a few careful smiles between Sarah and Amy and Robert when they were alone, but there were no wisecracks and William was glad of that. Mary Hand was special. You didn't imitate her raspy voice or make fun of her bossy manner. He'd grown up knowing that.

She *was* a bit on the bossy side—William would have admitted that—but when they all got adjusted, things were decidedly easier with Mary Hand a part of the family. She took over many of the chores that had made mornings a frantic rush to get everything done that needed doing before they left for school and work; she had the house in order and supper well on its way when they drove home in late afternoon; and, what was best of all, the two little girls loved her. Amy and Sarah appreciated all that; so did William—until Mary began talking about a subject that halted his good feeling for her as suddenly as the Volksie was sometimes braked at a danger spot.

The first stir of uneasiness came to him one day when he overheard her talking to Amy about Sarah.

"She has Jason's talent," Mary Hand was saying. "She simply must get more training. Now that I'm here to take over and you'll be next door to help me, there's no reason why we can't arrange to send her to some good school."

A little later Mary Hand let it slip that she had still other plans for Sarah. "She must get out and meet more people. John Hager tells me that she's had no social life whatever since she came down here. A girl her age should be meeting young men, not living like a hermit."

William raged to himself when he heard that. "Sure, if her precious Amy wants to get married, every other girl on earth must want to do the same—" He forgot his loyalty to Mary Hand; he wanted to ask her could she please let Sarah run her own life, could she just spend all her time thinking up nice things to do for Amy and leave Sarah alone.

He was reassured when Sarah shrugged off the idea of going away to school when Mary Hand talked to her about it.

"Can you imagine how I could leave three children, two dogs, a new bride, a huge garden, and a good job? No, thank you, Mary Hand. I have responsibilities around here and I have no intention of leaving them. Anyway, my work's not standing still; I get better with every picture I paint."

Mary Hand didn't say too much for a time, although William suspected she was doing plenty of thinking— getting a plan of action laid out. But other people were beginning to bug him with this talk about Sarah.

One afternoon when he went home with Johnny Hager after school for a round of handball, Johnny's mother took up Mary Hand's line of talk.

"We must get Sarah off to art school now that Mary's here, mustn't we, William?" Mrs. Hager said brightly when she brought out something cold for them to drink. "She has so much talent. Some of our friends who know a great deal about art say that she has the possibility of being as good or even better than her father."

Handball was no longer fun that day. Couldn't people, William wondered as he walked home, mind their own business? If Sarah wanted to go to art school, she'd make up her own mind, wouldn't she? It was a sure thing that she didn't need Mary Hand or the Hagers or their arty friends to tell her what she ought to do.

Even Robert had things to say that worried William. "Sarah's not living the kind of life a girl like her should be living. She's taken on responsibilities and settled down with them as if they make up her whole life. She's too young for that, William."

William remembered something Sarah had said to him. "She told me once that some things had happened in her life that made this place seem safe to her. She said it's something like a security blanket."

"Exactly," Robert answered, "and the time has come when she needs to throw security blankets in the clothes hamper and get out into the world. We've got to help her realize that."

It was the first time William had ever been really angry with Robert. *You* can help her to realize that, he thought bitterly, not me.

He resolutely pushed all these things people said about Sarah into the back of his mind; but they settled there and sulked and refused to leave his thoughts freed from a constant threat.

fourteen

ROBERT BROUGHT out plans for redoing the house next door. He'd spread them out on the floor of the living room and sit there explaining them to Amy and Sarah. He was putting a new roof over the whole house, laying new floors, building an extra bedroom and bath, restoring the fireplace which hadn't been used in years.

When Robert talked about the fireplace, he'd sit looking up at the portrait of Amy, seeming to study it intently. One such night Sarah smiled at Amy as if they shared a secret, and she said, "I've been thinking, Robert, that I'd like to give you that portrait for a wedding present if you'd like it. Of course if you'd rather have a seascape or one of my abstract works, I think I can get one done for you before the wedding."

Robert reached over and drew Sarah to his side. "I've wanted that painting ever since the first day I saw it, Sarah. I've wanted it because it's both Amy and you, and because it's so downright beautiful—" He leaned his head down and kissed her cheek. "Every day this fall whenever I'd think of getting the old fireplace rebuilt, I'd feel an ache for that portrait to hang over it."

And so when the girls selected material for draperies or curtains, when they looked at carpeting or lamps, they thought about the painting and tried to find colors that would pick up the colors on the canvas.

Robert worked hard during every hour he could spare from his landscaping work in town. He came out almost every evening and often he was sawing and pounding, plastering and painting, 'til as late as midnight. Amy and Sarah worked at sanding and waxing woodwork— especially the doors of the handsome cabinets Robert had built for the new kitchen. William helped with anything Robert wanted him to do, while Mary Hand in the other house sewed curtains and slipcovers that would make some of her old chairs look new for Amy's house.

It was a good time. Often when they had worked very late, the four of them would sit on the floor eating sandwiches, admiring their work or just yakking, never noticing the time or thinking how hard it would be to get up the next morning. William felt almost as old as Robert as he sat with them. One night they figured that in four years he'd be as tall as Robert—it felt good to be on a par with the three others.

When the fireplace in the living room had been rebuilt, Robert laid a slab of polished wood above it for a mantel and hung Amy's portrait over the mantel. Then they sat looking at it for a long time, noticing how it seemed to make the whole room glow.

"An original Sarah West," Amy said quietly. She put her hand on Sarah's as she spoke. William thought, A lot of water has run over the dam since that picture was painted. And then he thought, Well, good. Maybe the water has washed away a lot of troubles.

The little house was very pretty by spring. William liked the bright colors and the newness; he admitted to himself that Robert and Amy—with his help and Sarah's—had made the old rooms lovely. But it was also a strange house, one that might have been moved from town to among the orange trees at the edge of Pine Woods. It was another change around them, maybe a good one, but it was just one thing more that had been lost from the days when a family had lived there together. No point now in trying to believe that Mama might sometimes be there to listen to what he had to tell her—no point whatever. Mama would never recognize the place.

Amy and Mary Hand talked wedding plans until William tried to estimate how long he could survive as a hermit out in the woods beyond the sound of their voices. He was dismayed and disappointed in Robert, who would sit listening to wedding talk as if he actually enjoyed it. Even Sarah smiled at the talkers, although once in a while she gave William a secret look that told him she knew how he felt.

It took a long time for Amy to decide, but finally she did—sleeveless white cotton, that was the kind of dress she wanted. No veil, she said firmly when Mary Hand put up an argument; veils were for church weddings and she and Robert were going to be married out under the arch of jasmine that Robert had been training for months. She'd wear a low crown of white flowers—Sarah would know how to make it; Carla and Elizabeth must have crowns of many-colored flowers. Would Sarah wear one too? Amy wondered. But Sarah put a stop to that wondering. She said she'd wear a dress if Amy insisted, and maybe a brush of lipstick. But a crown of flowers? Definitely not. She made a face to show how much the very idea pained her. "I'd feel like a fool and look ludicrous, Amy," she said, and Amy looked at her wearily. Amy and Mary Hand raised their brows at one another, but they gave up talking about a crown of flowers for Sarah.

One day while Amy and Mary Hand talked on about their favorite subject, Sarah drove William and the little girls out to the quiet lake beyond the woods where they sometimes went for a swim. That was the day William asked Sarah about the trouble that was in his mind.

They watched over Elizabeth and Carla for a while as the girls paddled about in the shallow water and shrieked when they splashed one another. When the children were tired, Sarah helped them begin a sand castle and then climbed to a branch overhanging deep water where she and William could jump in for their swim.

He guessed his question surprised her somewhat because they'd been talking about many things, but not a word about weddings or anything like that. "Are you going to get married someday, Sarah?" he asked, and she laughed at his question.

"I haven't given it a lot of thought, William, but I don't think so—at least not for ten or fifteen years. There are so many other things I have to do—things that interest me more than getting married—"

She looked out across the lake and seemed to be thinking over the things she'd rather do. "I have to go on with my painting—that's important to me—and lately I've been planning how I could redecorate Mary Hand's old house if she is willing and we can scare up the money. I want to learn a lot more about gardening from Robert so Amy and I can build up a really beautiful garden; I must help Carla catch up with the schoolwork she has missed; and I'd like to find out if Elizabeth really has a talent for art or whether she just enjoys getting messed up with paint—" She stopped and looked at him with that straight, level look that was all Sarah's. "And maybe most of all, I want to watch you get through the next few years and grow into the kind of man I think you're going to be—" She laughed at him again. "So don't worry, William, I don't have a slot of space or time for taking on anything more."

She pushed him off the branch then and leaped into the water after him. They had a glorious swim that day and for a long time afterward, William felt lighthearted again.

The wedding, when it finally took place, was very nice. Thinking it over that night after Robert and Amy had gone away for their honeymoon, William thought Yes, as weddings go, Amy's had been all right.

The ceremony had been in late afternoon. The yard was cool and green, full of ladies in nice dresses and men in their best suits. Sarah and Carla stood beside Amy; William held tightly to Elizabeth's hand as they stood beside Robert. When the minister said that now Robert and Amy were husband and wife, the two little girls stepped up to Amy and offered her the flowers they'd been holding to put into her bridal bouquet. When they'd rehearsed, Amy had simply taken the flowers and smiled, but after the ceremony she suddenly grew tearful and knelt down to kiss each child. That almost got her into trouble because Elizabeth was so enthusiastic in the hug she gave Amy that Robert had to steady his bride or she would have toppled over. People laughed a little, but it was a very gentle kind of laughter.

Yes, the wedding had been nice, just the way Amy wanted it to be. And Amy was safe—over and over William told himself that Amy would be safe with Robert to look after her, to see that she didn't do flighty things, didn't get herself into trouble. Everything had worked out right, and William knew he should be happy. He would have been too, except for the things he'd heard people at the wedding say about Sarah.

"John Hager's friend, Hale Graham, is with the Art Institute in Chicago," William heard one lady say. "John says this man knew Jason West quite well. He's terribly interested in getting a scholarship for Sarah at the institute—"

And someone else said it was a pity that a girl with Sarah's gift should be down here working in a truck garden and taking care of children. And still another person thought that Sarah was wasting her youth. They all seemed to know they were right. They didn't call it breaking up a family—but it all added up to that.

William felt a coldness go up through his spine and when he thought no one would miss him, he left the company on the front lawn and went out to the woods by himself.

The sky was a deep blue, almost purple in the twilight, with a thousand stars scattered over it; but it was a lonesome sky that could make you ache if things were going wrong. He sat on his thinking stone and listened to the night noises for a while and to the laughter and buzz of talk up in the yard around Mary Hand's house. Then he sighed and whispered to himself, "We wouldn't be a family any longer if she left; we'd just be little pieces of a family waiting to see what was going to happen next."

He stared out into the dark forest. "I don't think that I could bear it," he told the night around him.

fifteen

"But don't you *want* to study, Sarah? Don't you want to follow in your father's footsteps?"

"Not all of them," Sarah answered shortly. She seated herself on a footstool and looked up into Mary Hand's face. "Jason, in all his tortured life, never found very many real satisfactions—*you* know that, Mary Hand. And I have. I've found many satisfactions right down here in these pine woods."

When Mary Hand said nothing, Sarah went on talking. "As I see it, I don't need to be in any great hurry. I've just turned twenty; it seems to me I could begin serious study in two or three years. It's possible to learn in later life, you know—" She seemed to be waiting for an objection to her words and when none came, she added, "My time isn't being wasted. I learn a lot from my mistakes—and just from the business of sitting down and trying—"

"But when an opportunity like this is staring you in the face, why wait for two or three more years?" Mary Hand asked, seeming almost to beg that Sarah be reasonable.

Sarah looked down at the floor for a while and when she answered, her words came slowly. "It would give all of us time to get a little stronger, time to make the jolt of breaking up the family a little less—you know—less whammo. Carla is still groping in a new world—"

"Amy can take care of Carla," Mary Hand interrupted.

"I'm very fond of Amy, Mary Hand, but I think I understand Carla's problems better than Amy does. Call it egotism, if you will, but that's the way I feel about it—"

"I call it looking for an excuse to stay here and let chances for a better future slide right by you," Mary Hand said severely.

Sarah didn't answer for a minute during which she watched Elizabeth busily at work on a coloring book as she lay flat on the living room floor. "And another thing," she continued slowly, "my mother deserted me when I was a baby—at least she deserted Jason and left me with him. I've never been conscious of missing her much except occasionally when I've seen girls my age feeling very close to their mothers. At times like that I've felt that perhaps I've missed something important in my life. I don't want Elizabeth to feel that way—"

"Well, good Heavens, Sarah, you're not deserting her. You're leaving her for a few months with people who love her as much as you do. When she's old enough for school you may be able to take her with you—"

"If I take Elizabeth, I'll take Carla too—and William—" Sarah was getting angry; William knew the signs.

"That, I'm afraid, would have to be considered carefully. Carla and William don't belong to you. Sarah—"

"They belonged to me when they needed to be kept together and loved because they hadn't a relative on earth or a home. They've belonged to me for four years, Mary Hand. Those children are mine—don't tell me that they aren't—"

Sarah wasn't crying, but one dry sob burst out of her throat and the sound of it seemed to make Mary Hand sorry. Suddenly she looked very gentle and smoothed Sarah's hair. "I'll not say another word about your leaving, Sarah. If you want to stay down here with your little family, it's all right with me—"

William felt a great relief. If Mary got off Sarah's neck, maybe they could forget about her going away.

But he soon found out that there were others just as dangerous to his peace of mind as Mary Hand had been. Johnny's parents drove out late one afternoon with a letter they wanted Sarah to see.

"It's the most fabulous news, Sarah. Wait until you read what John's friend at the Art Institute in Chicago has to say in this letter—" William thought of how he had always rather liked Johnny's mother—a pleasant, friendly lady, but lately as irritating as a determined mosquito.

They left the letter with Sarah and later when she had read it twice over, she looked up and found William staring at her. She shook her head and the look she gave him was sad. Then she handed the letter to him.

He didn't understand all of it, but he got enough from what someone in Chicago had written to send his fears rampaging through him again.

"I found the material in the portfolio you sent me shows outstanding ability. The influence of her father is, of course, quite apparent, but she has a style that is uniquely her own. It will give me pleasure to welcome Jason West's daughter to the Art Institute—"

There was more. These people in Chicago would pay for Sarah's studies through a scholarship. That was what Mr. Hager was talking about when he said, "We've been proud of you, Sarah, all along. Now this opportunity comes up and we're thrilled—really thrilled. Not many young people your age are going to have this chance— not many deserve it—"

That night Sarah sat in the big armchair in the living room and just looked at William and the little girls. Finally she spoke to Carla and Elizabeth. "Would you mind if Sarah went to Chicago so she can learn to be a better artist? I'd be home for vacations, you know—maybe for weeks during the summer—"

Elizabeth began to whimper and Carla threw herself across Sarah's lap. "You're our Sarah," Elizabeth cried, "you belong to us," and Carla repeated, "Don't leave us—please don't leave us, Sarah—"

William thought, Cry, girls, cry hard. Make her see that she can't leave you.

But just at that moment Robert stepped up to the door, and things changed in a flash. "Are there two little girls here who would like to drive into town with Amy and me for ice-cream cones?" he asked. "Or a young man either?" he added, looking at William.

The girls were immediately out of the door, screaming their delight, forgetting all about Sarah leaving for Chicago. William shook his head at Robert.

Sarah watched the children skipping along on either side of Robert. "Well, that's how Sarah stacks up against ice cream," she said, taking a long breath. "Didn't *you* want a scoop of something cool this hot night?"

"I couldn't swallow it," he answered. He walked out of the room into the yard where the dogs were waiting for a walk.

Robert and Amy were very kind to Sarah in the way they talked to her about taking advantage of the scholarship Mr. Hager's friend was offering her.

"We love you, Sarah, and of course we'll miss you," Amy said, "but Robert and I think this is a chance in a lifetime—"

"As for the children," Robert went on, "you've had the responsibility of them for a long time, and you've worked yourself to the bone for them. Surely Amy and I can take over now with Mary Hand's help—"

"There's William," Sarah said, glancing over at the window where William pretended to be uninterested in the conversation. "There are a lot of adjustments to make in the first year of high school—"

"William is practically a young man, Sarah," Robert answered. "He and I are pretty good friends—I may understand his problems, if he has any, even better than you would—"

Sarah's voice was suddenly harsh. "You two don't seem to realize that what other people call a 'recluse' suits me just fine; you can't seem to realize that painting when and what and how I want to paint and taking care of the kids I love are things that are quite all right with me. Everybody feels that they—not I—know what I should do—make a name for myself; make my work measure up to Jason's in the eyes of the critics, meet some man, for God's sake, and get myself married—" She stood glaring at Robert and Amy. "Look, Robert, I think you're great—I'm glad Amy loves you and you're both blessed by clergy. But let me tell you something: I want to be married as much as—as I want a girly-girly dress with a feather boa around my neck—"

"You must weigh values, Sarah," Amy said weakly.

"I do weigh values, Amy. It's just that you and Robert and Mary Hand and the Hagers—it's just that all of you put different weights on the things I value—"

Mary Hand didn't do any more talking to Sarah, but she took William aside one day. "You mustn't let Sarah see how much you hate for her to leave, William. It's leaving you that hurts her more than anything else. She knows the little girls will soon get over missing her. But your eyes, William—it just about kills Sarah when she looks at those big sad eyes of yours—"

And one day when he drove into town with Robert for the Saturday work, Robert spoke to him about showing his feelings.

"She ought to go, William—she knows very well

she should. But when she sees the sadness in your face, she cracks up. Maybe you can do a little playacting. You'd be doing it for her own good—"

And so that evening as they worked together giving Nugget her bath and brushing snarls out of her hair, William tried to act the way Robert thought it was right for him to act.

Sarah had been silent for a long time and she didn't look up when she finally spoke. "How would it strike you, William, if I just tell people that I don't give a rap what any of them think—that I simply am not of a mind to leave here right now?"

He found it hard to answer her. He wanted to say, Why don't you do that, Sarah? Why don't you say that you guess you can make up your mind, that you don't need advice from any of them?

But, then, everybody thought that Sarah ought to go—that it was for her own good. Mary Hand thought so, of course; most important, Robert thought so. If William believed in anyone other than Sarah, it was Robert.

"I'd think," he said, almost choking on his words, "that you're more your own boss than little Carla was. She didn't want to go to Boston, but all of us were big. We made her go because we thought we knew what was right for her. Robert carried her on the plane, but nobody's going to carry *you* on a big jet headed for Chicago."

Sarah laid Nugget's hairbrush down in a quick movement. "Oh, William," she said, and her voice sounded as though he had struck her.

She left the rest of Nugget's grooming to William and walked out into the yard, stopping to look at every bush and flowering plant, examining a flower held closely in her hands as if she might be thinking of painting it. When William released a freshly bathed Nugget, the big dog raced to Sarah, frisking at her feet, and she put her head down to look into Nugget's brown eyes. She was still out in the yard when darkness came, and then William joined her timidly—not sure that she wanted him.

"Are you mad at me, Sarah?" he asked in a low voice.

She took his hand and they walked together down the path toward the woods. After they'd gone a little distance she said, "Have I ever been mad at you, William?"

He shook his head. "I don't think so," he said.

She looked at him soberly. "I guess I had to hear it from you before I was jolted into action. That's because I know you love me a little more than any of the others do. Elizabeth and Carla love me, but they forget quickly. You are the one who is going to be hurt most at our family breaking up, so if you say I should go, I somehow know I must."

"But you won't be leaving forever, Sarah. After you've learned to paint as well as your father—maybe better—you'll come back and we can all be a family again—you and me and the little girls with Amy and Robert next door—"

Sarah stood looking off through the woods for a long time. Then she repeated some words very slowly, words he'd never heard before:

". . . as all things flow, nothing abides. Into the same river one cannot step twice—"

"Do you understand that, William?" she asked after a minute.

"No," he said. "It sounds nice though—like a poem—"

"A Greek named Heraclitus wrote it centuries ago. It means—well, just what it says. Nothing—our bodies, our minds, our relationships with others—nothing will ever stay the same. Not even the waters in a river—"

"I don't like to think of things being like that—"

"I know, but we have to face it. We like to believe that things will always be the same—at least those things that are warm and good. But they won't, William. We have to grow up and face some unpleasant facts—"

"A lot of unpleasant things have happened for you to face down here. I don't know why you'd want to stay—"

"I do though. Because so many things, more good than bad, have changed my life—all kinds of things that make me want to settle down here and stay on and on. But I won't. I'll come back for Elizabeth one of these days—she's my child and I must take care of her. I'd like to take Carla too if you and Amy and Robert will agree to it—and, of course, if Carla *wants* to come with me. I'd like to have her and Elizabeth grow up together—" She looked straight into his eyes the way she'd looked when she was getting ready to paint his portrait. "As for you, William, well, you'll soon be a young man—you'll have school and sports and hard work; you'll have your palomino and girls like Carole to think about. I suppose it's better for you to be here with Amy and Robert. It's awfully hard for me to accept that, but I guess it's better—"

They didn't say anything more, but when they got to the house William asked her to write down the words Heraclitus had said about things changing. He read them over several times and put them with some other things that were important to him.

As the week went by all the plans were made. Johnny's father called his friend in Chicago, and then he called Sarah to tell her that Mr. Graham would meet her, that he'd found a pleasant place for her to live.

And so on Friday Robert drove Sarah into town

where she would board a bus for Chicago. Everyone—the Hagers, Robert and Amy, Mary Hand—all of them urged Sarah to fly, but she wouldn't.

"I don't have much money," she said, "and I'm not going to begin this new chapter by putting myself in debt. Anyway," she smiled at all of them—the old mischievous, almost defiant smile they used to see on her face so often—"I can get off a bus much easier than a jet if I change my mind and decide to come back and live as I please." Watching her, William's heart skipped with a sudden hope.

Carla and Elizabeth cried a little when Sarah kissed them good-bye, but they were cheered when Amy asked if they'd like to bake cookies in her new kitchen and send a box of them to Sarah as soon as she reached Chicago. They hugged Sarah, kissed her over and over, and then ran together across the yard to the house next door. Watching them from the window, Sarah's eyes looked sad; then she seemed to pull herself together and turned to kiss Amy and Mary Hand good-bye.

William walked with Sarah out to the driveway. It's like another hurricane is brewing, he thought, like Amy telling me Dr. Finley said Mama would soon die, it's like maybe the whole bottom of the world is falling out underneath me—

"Do you want to drive into town with us, William?" Robert called from the car where he was getting Sarah's luggage piled inside.

William shook his head. "No," he said.

Sarah stopped a few feet from the car, and William thought, This is it— He held out his hand the way Mr. Cooper did when he said good-bye to her, but instead of shaking hands, Sarah suddenly put her arms around his shoulders and pressed her cheek to his. "Thank you for letting me share Mama's name for you," she whispered.

Then she added, "I'm going to miss you, Sweet William—"

It was a lonely afternoon and evening. At twilight Carla and Elizabeth came running over to ask Mary Hand if they could stay all night with Amy and Robert. They looked at the silent rooms and William thought once that they were going to cry. But the fun of staying over at Amy's, at being the first to sleep in the freshly decorated guest room cheered them, and they ran off upstairs to collect their toothbrushes and nightgowns—chattering as they would have done if Sarah had been at home, a part of the family, someone they'd learned to depend upon.

Mary Hand looked at him. "I guess there's not much point in my cooking supper tonight, is there, William?" and he told her no, there was no point in it.

After a while he took a walk through the woods with Nugget, deep into the thickest part and finally over to the little lake where he and Sarah had talked together, where they swam and William had laughed and felt lighthearted after Sarah had told him all the reasons why she was not going away. He thought once about taking a swim with Nugget, but it didn't seem to be worth the effort. So he turned and walked back to the house, which by then was dark and silent with emptiness. He could hear Mary Hand talking out on the porch next door. She had grown lonely, he guessed, and decided to visit with Amy and Robert.

William was not yet ready to go to bed. He piled the cushions on the living room couch into one corner and curled up among them as he had that night long ago when he and Sarah made plans for going ahead at the job of living, and that, William thought, was what he must do now.

There was his steady work with Robert on Saturdays;

on other days there was school and a hurried trip home to work in the garden, to fertilize citrus trees and trim bushes; there was helping Carla learn to read as Sarah had been doing every day since she and Carla came home from Boston. There were deep-sea fishing trips to take with Robert when they had the time. And first, last, and always, there was Blue Streak. Another year and maybe he'd be able to buy a palomino like the one Papa had promised him before the accident at work.

He closed his eyes and thought maybe he could go to sleep, but he kept thinking of that bus on a long highway leading to Chicago. He imagined he could see Sarah leaning her head against the back of her seat, her big eyes wide open and staring out at the night. He wondered if once in a while she thought of how easy it would be to get off the bus and board a southbound one back home.

When Mary Hand came in and found him on the couch she touched his shoulder. "Hadn't you better get to bed, William?" she asked. And he told her yes, that he would be going up to his room in a few minutes.

But he forgot. He was tired and sleep came to him without warning so that he fell back among the pillows and knew nothing more for hours.

It must have been in the small hours of morning that the dream came to him, so clear and vivid, so much like real life that he awoke trembling with excitement. It showed him a picture of night just turning into dawn, and of a big blue and silver bus pulling up in front of the station in town. A long line of people, looking rumpled and sleepy, began coming down the steps of the bus when the driver opened the door; somewhere mixed up in the dream, William heard Sarah's voice just before he woke up. She was telling him how easy it was to get off a bus and come back to paint and take care of the kids she loved. Her voice sounded like she didn't care what Mary Hand or the Hagers or Robert and Amy thought— she was simply coming back to do as she pleased.

He got up in the darkness, still fully dressed, and groped his way to the front door. There wasn't any question in his mind about what he must do. The dream had been more than just an ordinary dream—it had been vivid and clear; there was a command in it, something that said, "Pay attention. This is for real."

Outside Nugget whimpered and wanted to go with him, but he whispered to her and made her lie down beside Duchess. Then he went out to the road and started toward town.

He had made that walk to town so many times he couldn't possibly have guessed how many—sometimes in the blistering heat, sometimes in the rain, sometimes on a bright day with a breeze blowing and the trees along the road making cool shadows in the dust. But he had never been out on it so early before. He wasn't afraid, just conscious of a strangeness all around him and inside him.

The big clock inside the bus station said a quarter to four. There was no one behind the window in the ticket office, no other person around the place. William stretched out on one of the wooden benches and dropped off contentedly to sleep again.

There was a pale light outside when the ticket agent came in. "You waiting for the southbound bus from Atlanta?" he asked.

"Yes," William answered. He couldn't be sure, but that sounded as if it might very well be the one.

"Got your ticket?"

"No. Just here to meet someone."

The man nodded. "Well she's due here in a few minutes. They'll unload out in front of the station."

William shook himself briskly and walked outside as the bus drew up. It was blue and silver, just as it had been in his dream.

The driver got out first, looking rumpled and dusty, but cheerful as he held out a hand to help people step down. "Café right across the street," he was telling people. "Time for a cup of coffee before we leave for Miami."

A woman got off first, carrying a baby and almost dragging a sleepy little girl who was crying. An old man followed her, touching each step carefully with his cane before he put a foot down. A well-dressed man, dignified as Mr. Hager, got off next, and then two girls with big purses hanging from their shoulders. They kept getting off the bus, a long line of people, but finally the line ended and the driver closed the bus door. William stepped up to him.

"Is everybody off?" he asked.

"Every last one of them," the driver said. "Why? Didn't your party show up?"

When William looked at the ground without speaking, the driver laid a hand on his shoulder. "Sorry, kid," he said, "I hope nothing's wrong—"

"No," William answered, managing a smile. "I wasn't much expecting her anyway."

He walked to the other side of the station and looked up at the sky where sunrise was touching every cloud in the east with colors Sarah would have known how to get down on her canvas. He was tired, but that didn't matter; tiredness was nothing compared to his chagrin and bewilderment. The dream which was nothing more than a teasing lie had been so clear, so lifelike; and once it had come to him, he couldn't have spent the rest of the night at home remembering how Sarah had carried her

186

luggage from the station four years ago and had fainted at Mary Hand's front steps.

"I *had* to come over and meet that bus," he told himself, but he felt a low burn of anger that he had been tricked by someone or something—just who or what, he couldn't be sure.

Of course I was a fool to believe she'd change her mind, he thought after a minute. Not Sarah—she's not like that.

All at once he was glad—glad that she hadn't come back looking ashamed of being wishy-washy, of not being able to make up her mind and stick to it. He would like to tell whatever or whoever had prompted his dream, that he was proud of Sarah for never giving a second thought to getting off that northbound bus and coming home.

Things were beginning to grow clearer in his mind; he knew somehow that there had been a change inside him since that last passenger stepped off the bus.

Then he remembered. Change. That was something Sarah had told him about, something that he suddenly realized was all around him and his family. Mama gone. Amy a married lady. Carla with eyes that could see. Elizabeth saying, "I want pig-tails, Amy. I'm getting too big for curls."

And Sarah. She'd be living in a strange city, learning new things, meeting new people. Never quite the same Sarah who sat with a little boy one lonely night and tried to ease his heartbreak. "Into the same river" came to his mind; as he started toward home the words kept coming back, over and over like a tune you don't really want to sing, but insists on coming to your lips when you're not thinking.

His step grew firmer as he went along the familiar

road, still shadowy in the early light. Sarah had known what she was talking about; so had old Heraclitus centuries ago. "As all things flow," he whispered to himself, "nothing abides. Into the same river one cannot step twice."

He was not happy, but he felt strong enough to force unhappiness back, to face things as they were. He smiled ever so slightly, the smile being reluctant about coming to his lips.

I'll tell her all about this sometime, he thought. She'll laugh, but she'll understand. It will be something just between the two of us—